PRAISE FOR SAUL WILLIAMS AND
THE DEAD EMCEE SCROLLS

"Saul Williams is the prototype synthesis between poetry and hip-hop, stage and page, rap and prose, funk and mythology, slam and verse . . . he avoids classifications, and empowers the human voice. All of this is represented in Williams's newest book, *The Dead Emcee Scrolls*."

—Mark Eleveld, author of *The Spoken Word Revolution: Slam,
Hip-Hop and the Poetry of the Next Generation*

"Once again one of the finest minds in the country has put pen to paper, voice to verse, and dug into the deep, rich planet better known as the souls of black folks."

—Nelson George, author of *Hip-Hop America*

"One of the most inspiring voices in American hip-hop."

—Trent Reznor, Nine Inch Nails

"An astonishing . . . poet. The internal rhyme, metrics, and imagery are so fleet . . . that they're humbling."

—*The Washington Post*

"Hip-hop's poet laureate . . . Saul Williams isn't out to save hip-hop, but he is out to elevate the art form [and] is effectively breaking boundaries while blurring the line between poetry and rap."

—CNN

"[Saul Williams] is a mighty talent. He takes readers on epic voyages into frontiers that offer a refreshing awakening of the mind and a roller coaster ride into an abyss of demons, deities, occult symbols, and more."

—*Amsterdam News*

SAUL WILLIAMS, one of America's bestselling poets, is the author of three previous books of poetry: *, said the shotgun to the head* and $S\sqrt{he}$ (both from MTV Books/Pocket Books) and *The Seventh Octave* (Moore Black Press). His music albums, *Amethyst Rock Star* and *Saul Williams,* earned him great critical acclaim, as did his starring role in *Slam*. Williams also cowrote that film, which garnered the Grand Jury Prize at the Sundance Film Festival and the Camera D'or at the Cannes Film Festival.

THE
DEAD EMCEE
SCROLLS

THE LOST TEACHINGS OF HIP-HOP
AND CONNECTED WRITINGS

SAUL WILLIAMS

POCKET BOOKS

NEW YORK   LONDON   TORONTO   SYDNEY

POCKET BOOKS, a division of Simon & Schuster, Inc.
1230 Avenue of the Americas, New York, NY 10020

ISBN-13: 978-1-4165-1632-3
ISBN-10:   1-4165-1632-8

This MTV Books/Pocket Books trade paperback edition February 2006

10   9   8   7   6   5

Manufactured in the United States of America

For information regarding special discounts for bulk purchases,
please contact Simon & Schuster Special Sales at 1-800-456-6798 or
business@simonandschuster.com

This book is dedicated
to the dedicated:
Afronauts of over-
crammed space, those of
sewed-in creases and
ironed shoelaces, Gazelle
framed screw-faces.
Way before court cases
were platinum sales,
quest for mix-tapes like
the Holy Grail. Retro
earthquake fitting.
Metro landmark bidding.
NGHs was wiggin out!
Newburgh know what
I'm talking bout. B-
boys! B-girls!
Caesars and Jheri curls.
This book is dedicated
to the under-rated
hustler, high school
dropouts, school dance
shoot-outs, NGHs with
Uzis! Bitches and
floozies!
This book is dedicated to
y'all too! Pull your
panties up and feel me!
Help me, lord. Heal me.
This book is dedicated to
the Sunday preacher:
the original pimped out,
laid back hustler, with
God on his side and
Italian leather in his ride.
Toot your horn
and feel me.
This book is dedicated to
the sho nuff sho nuff.
The nappy dugout:
corn-rowed, twisted and
braided and the NGH
who parlayed it into cold
cash. NGH, you crazy!
I'm 'a sick my dogs on
you.

This book is dedicated to those who prayed for it, who saw it before it was here, who sensed it from the beginning.
This book is dedicated to the beginning. Before before and right now.
This book is dedicated to the lunch table. The boom bap. I still got my 12 inch of Spoonin Rap! To all the original blueprints. I know ya heard of that!
This book is dedicated to yellow caps in Lemon Heads boxes (Krak Attack!), three quarter bombers, and Africans selling time machines in Times Square by moonlight (clear nail polish on fake gold will make it last longer. Ain't nobody talkin bout diamonds. Not yet.
But this book is dedicated to that too!). Name belts, name rings, name-plates, gold ropes, door knocker earrings, and gold fronts. This book is dedicated to that more than once.
This book is dedicated to Phillie blunts, Oakland Raider jackets, "X" caps, Spike's Joint, and a bunch of shit that became corny overnight. This book is dedicated to those that write! Fab 5, Futura, Doze, shake your cans and feel me!

This book is dedicated to floor wizards spinning on backs, head, and hands, and cute girls that ain't afraid to dance.

But, nah, it ain't only about the old school. This book is dedicated to platinum grills and apple bottoms. Backpackers in Benzes with white Jesus medallions and his crown of diamond thorns hanging from their necks. Hardy har har, NGHs. Change clothes and feel me.

This book is dedicated to moguls, def to death. Please don't take a shit on the chest of our generation (Vicelord, your majesty). Ugly NGHs with money to burn. The ass thou pimpest shall be thine own. Funk God I know you feel me. Now let me hold a li'l something so I can get the IRS off my back (I can't always bring myself to pay taxes to a government that uses our money to steal more land and ignore the ongoing plight of the poor in our names! What's realer than that?). All this money is dirty. You can't buy freedom, but let's buy some airtime and shelf-space and elevate this freedom of speech.

Free your mind, brother. Peaceful Pimpin'

since '72. Ask my baby
mamas, they'll tell ya.
What? You never heard
of that?
This book is dedicated to
Crunchy Black,
Willie D, Face, Kane,
and all you dark-skinned
cats that had to smile to
be seen.
This book is dedicated to
freedom, although it
comes at a cost.
Don't steal it, y'all
("steal" should read
"find" if the subject is
white, in which case
the subject is free
to help himself).
This book is dedicated to
white people, 'cause y'all
feel it too. All these
so-called races. What we
runnin' for? Don't believe
the hype! We are one.
This book is dedicated to
greater understanding,
power, and NGHs with
enough game to flaunt it.
This book is dedicated to
Yahshua Clay (You know
who you is NGH, Stand
up!), Niggy Tardust,
Tennessee Slim
(Detonate!), Soggy Lama
III (and the sirens of
Atlantis that sing his
praises), Zupert Henry
(your mamas car ain't
faster than mine, boy),
Rebekka Holylove (hip
hip shalom!), and the
luminous heroes of
today, now, and

forevermore (I hold
my nuts as I exit)!

P.S. Did you know the
mothership was built in
Newburgh, NY? That's
what I be meanin when I
say "Word to the Mother."
Selah.

In the final analysis,
every generation must be responsible
for itself.

PAUL ROBESON

A CONFESSION

There is no music more powerful than hip-hop. No other music so purely demands an instant affirmative on such a global scale. When the beat drops, people nod their heads, "yes," in the same way that they would in conversation with a loved one, a parent, professor, or minister. Instantaneously, the same mechanical gesture that occurs in moments of dialogue as a sign of agreement which subsequently, releases increased oxygen to the brain and, thus, broadens one's ability to understand, becomes the symbolic and actual gesture that connects you to the beat. No other musical form has created such a raw and visceral connection to the heart while still incorporating various measures from other musical forms that then appeal to other aspects of the emotional core of an individual. Music speaks directly to the subconscious. The consciously simplified beat of the hip-hop drum speaks directly to the heart. The indigenous drumming of continental Africa is known to be primarily dense and quite often up-tempo. The drumming of the indigenous Americas, on the other hand, in its most common representation is primarily sparse and down-tempo. What happens when you put a mixer and cross-fader between those two cultural realities? What kind of rhythms and polyrhythms might you come up with? Perhaps one complex yet basic enough to synchronize the hearts of an entire generation.

To program a drumbeat is to align an external rhythmic device to an individual's biorhythm. I remember being introduced to the hip hop/electronica sub-genre, drum and bass, by one of its pioneers, Goldie. I accompanied him to his DJ set at the London club, the Blue Note. After about an hour of him staring straight into my eyes, gold teeth glaring, miming or pointing to every invisible, yet highly audible, bass line, kick, snare, and high hat, he took me outside and instructed me to monitor my heartbeat so that I might note that the intensity of the music in the club had actually sped it up so that my heart was, now, pounding—a sort of high speed drum and bass metronome. I had been re-programmed (note: it was a high-speed wireless connection). Did it affect how I thought? I don't know, but surely, the potential was there. The music of that night had been mostly without lyrics. But if there were lyrics, could they have affected me on a subconscious level in the same way that the music itself had affected me on a subatomic level? Who knows? What I do know is that I have been a hip hop head for years. I have nodded my head to the music that initially affirmed my existence as an African American male. And then, of course, as the music grew more openly misogynistic and capitalistic, I found myself being a bit more picky about exactly what I would choose to nod my head to. It was difficult. Sometimes the beats were undeniable. Regardless, even though

I always sensed the power of the music, even though I remember the few hip-hop songs that brought tears to my eyes because they went beyond speaking of the power of the music and hinted at the power of our generation, nothing, absolutely nothing could have prepared me for the story that I am about to share.

I have paraded as a poet for years now. In the process of parading I may have actually become one, but that's another story, another book. This book is a book that I have been waiting to finish since 1995. This is the book that finished me. The story I am about to tell may sound fantastic. It may anger some of you who have followed my work. You may feel that you have come to know me over the years, and in some cases you have, but in others . . . well, this is a confession.

I came to New York in 1994, having just graduated from Morehouse College in Atlanta, Georgia, where I had majored in philosophy and drama. I was about to begin my first year in the graduate acting program at NYU. I was very excited. I had been planning my career as an actor my entire life and everything was going exactly as planned. Because I could study drama in school, it was never simply a hobby for me; it was a professional choice. On the other hand, I had been rapping for as long as I had been acting, but rapping was never something I could study in school. It was extra curricular. I wrote rhymes between classes (and often during). I battled at lunchtime and recess. It was my favorite past time.

Time passed and by the time I graduated from college I no longer wrote rhymes. I was becoming more focused on acting. Yet, the time that I once spent writing rhymes was now spent listening and critiquing hip-hop. I was a purist. I saw my list of the top ten emcees as *the* list. I could talk hip-hop all day. And not just the music, the culture. I had been a breakdancer and had even spent part of my time in Atlanta dancing for an up-and-coming rap group. Junior high and high school had been hardly more than a fashion show for me: Lee suits, name belts, name rings, fat laces, you name it. Growing up just an hour outside of New York City had kept me feverishly close to the culture. We always did our back to school shopping on Farmers Boulevard in the Bronx, 8th Street in Manhattan, Dr. Jays in Harlem, Delancey, Orchard and any other place mentioned in classic hip-hop songs to make sure we were never behind the trends. I'm tempted to list the color of my sheep skin, Pumas, shell toes, Lottos, Filas, how many Lees I had, sewed in creases, fat laces, name rings, truck jewelry. What?! Unfuck-witable. Its really the only reason why despite any career success I may experience I hardly bling. I blang.

I never really tried to DJ, but I definitely tried my hand as a graffiti writer. I was never any good, but I always had the utmost respect for any kid that could "write," as we used to say. I used to watch my cousin Duce and my man Sergio practice their alphabet everyday. As graff writers they knew that every aspect of their writing had to be original. They would transform their letters into highly stylistic, barely legible testaments of ghetto inventiveness. I would try, but I sucked and I knew it. So usually, I just focused on writing rhymes. But my admiration for the art of graffiti writing remained intact. So intact that when I moved to the City for grad school and a friend mentioned that he knew some hidden spots where some legendary graffiti existed and offered to take me on a tour following sub-way tracks to caverns between stations, I urged him to take me immediately.

Flashlight in hand, we descended the platform and ventured into the darkness. The mazes we journeyed were womblike and seemed infinite. I had to get used to the rats venturing between the rails. I was having flashbacks of *Beat Street* and *Wild Style*, two films that practically defined my youth. I remembered the word "Spit" popping up over detailed graffiti. The ultimate dis, defacement of defacement. My mind ventured to the present where so many emcees and poets were now using the word "spit" instead of rap or rhyme. "Yo, let me spit over that track." Graffiti culture still resonates deeply in the heart of hip-hop, whether we realize it or not. I remember learning of ancient Egyptian dynasties and how, in some, the scribes were more popular, while in others the focus was on the illustrators. Depending on the dynasty or pharaoh of an age, the work on the walls of a pyramid may have more words and scriptures versus more illustrations of the words and scriptures. This topic always made me think of the subject of beats vs. rhymes and early nineties hip-hop, ushered in by Dr. Dre and *The Chronic*. It was the first time I ever heard people overtly appreciating beats and flow over content. I remember not knowing whether to fast forward or play "Bitches Ain't Shit" (to me, one of the dopest tracks on the album, especially because of "The Bridge" sample) while in mixed company. Some people, women in particular, would be instantly offended, while others excused the lyrics because of Snoop's intoxicating flow. It became common to hear people say, almost apologetically, "Oh, I just like the beat." One of my professors at the time, Pearl Cleage, now a renowned novelist, had come out with a book called *Mad at Miles,* which she shared in class. In the book she spoke of not being able to listen to Miles Davis's softly muted trumpet without hearing the muted screams of the women he had unabashedly abused. She opened my eyes to misogyny and the way it plays out in our daily life. I wrote a horrible play for her class attempting to address the issue of misogyny in hip-hop. *The Chronic* was number one on the charts at the time. And just as I began to think about how Ms. Cleage and her class had deeply affected me, we reached the first stop on our underground graffiti tour. The first stop changed my life.

A piece had been painted that, to this day, I don't really know how to describe. It looked three dimensional, as if the letters had been painted on top of each other instead of side by side. They seemed to be exiting a wide-open mouth, like bullets from a chamber. I remember stepping closer for a better look and kicking one of many spray paint cans. This one, however, was heavy as if it were full. Excited by the possibility of leaving my tag, I picked it up. Almost immediately, I realized its heaviness was not the sort that one would expect from liquid. I then shook the can and heard a shuffle-like movement. I removed the top, expecting to find a spray nozzle. Instead, what I found was what appeared to be tightly coiled pieces of paper. Almost immediately, I placed the top back on the can as if I had seen nothing unusual, removed my backpack and slid it inside. I assume my friend thought I was keeping a souvenir for myself. He didn't ask and I didn't explain. For whatever reasons I had immediately determined to discover the contents of my find alone.

At home that evening, I removed the can from my bag and attempted to liberate its contents. It was an aged yellowish-brown paper that reminded me of the homemade paper that my college roommate's crafty girlfriend would sometimes make out of recycled goods. I pinched the sides and without much difficulty removed it from the can. As soon as I did, instead of staying together as I expected, part of the scroll's center fell to the ground. I noted that it had rolled under my chair and began a more careful process of opening the remainder. I began to uncoil the manuscript and soon found that it was not one long scroll, but several scrolled pages rolled together. The first page was the longest. I immediately attempted to read what was written on it and found that I could not make out the words. They seemed to be written with great care, yet almost appeared to be written in a foreign alphabet like Arabic, Sanskrit, or Hebrew. If this was the work of a graffiti artist, it was highly advanced and practically academic. I may have spent about twenty minutes looking at that first page, unable to decipher a single word. I rolled it up and then, one by one, unrolled the other pages and saw that they were all written in the same hand. I placed them back together, rolled them tightly and returned them back to the can. I then picked up the one page that had rolled under my chair, carried it with me to my bed and uncoiled it. It was no different than the others. The writing, though artfully crafted, seemed illegible. After a few minutes of staring at it, I began to form the opinion that it was not written in a foreign alphabet. It was someone's personal alphabet, like the ones Duce and Sergio would create. But this "someone" was surely a master. It felt old. Older than something written in the eighties or even the seventies. It felt ancient. If I had found it in a museum, I'm not certain that I would have linked it with graffiti. But finding it in a spray can in a graffiti site put it in an unusual context. Yet, not unusual enough to think that it didn't belong there. Somehow, it felt connected. It made sense. But I could make no sense of it. I stared long and hard, amazed that an individual's penmanship could be so ancient and "street." I began to think of it like a piece of graffiti. How many times had I stood looking at a wall trying to decipher a graff writer's work of art? We would pride ourselves on being the first to decipher a piece. And the best pieces always had to be deciphered. But this piece was like no other. I traced the first word with my finger, turned it upside down, and squinted my eyes. I tried every trick I could think of, yet nothing worked. My eyes grew tired. I left that one page of the manuscript on my night table and went to sleep. I didn't look at it again for over a week.

In the week that passed I started my graduate acting training at NYU. It was going to be three years of intensive study. To my surprise, the only book that we were required to have was a journal. We were told that no one would read our journals. The professors simply wanted to know that we were recording our thoughts and experiences and guaranteed us that we would thank them for the requirement. I had never really kept a journal and was excited about beginning. I went to Urban Outfitters and found a pocket-sized brown journal with yellow lined pages, and an elastic strap to keep it closed. It cost me five bucks. I loved it. For whatever reasons I had begun to put great thought into what my first words would be in this new journal. It was as if I was beginning a series of letters to my unborn children by keeping it and I wanted to pay particular attention to what I wrote. The blank journal stayed in my pocket for days.

At home one night before going to bed I placed the journal on my nightstand beside the scrolled page of the manuscript. I had recently begun the practice of sitting in silence and doing a five-minute meditation before going to sleep. I would sit on the floor, cross my legs, straighten my spine, close my eyes, and focus my thoughts by simply focusing on following my breath as it came in through my nose, traveled down to my diaphragm, and then exited my mouth. A certain peace prevailed when I did this. It also seemed to help me remember my dreams. This night, after meditating, I climbed in bed and decided to look at the manuscript page. Once again, I was amazed at the craft of the writing. It was slowly beginning to settle on me that this text was old. Pyramid old. But it still felt graffiti connected. Rather than getting frustrated at my inability to decipher the text, I was gaining more appreciation for the genius of whoever had written this. Almost without thinking about it, I picked up the blank journal and the pen beside it. I propped the manuscript page open on the bed beside me and attempted to copy the first few words into my journal. What happened next is hard to describe. I figured I would keep my eyes on the manuscript while copying my rendition into my journal. It was a subconscious decision. My focus was on looking at the details of the writing and copying it without looking at my hand or what I was writing or how it looked. I kept my eyes on the manuscript page while my hand worked at crafting a copy into my journal without peeking at my own handy work. I copied what seemed to be the first phrase or sentence and then allowed myself to look at what I had written. To my surprise, what I had copied was hardly as illegible as the original. I expected to find awkward scribbles, instead what I found was a sloppily written sentence, which read, **"I stand on the corner of the block slingin' amethyst rocks."** I looked back at the manuscript, and, yes, the first phrase was now somehow legible to me. I could see clearly that that was indeed what it said. However I could not as easily decipher the following phrase. It appeared that I was going to have to go through the process of copying without peeking again. I did. When I finished copying the next phrase, I looked at my journal and read **"Drinkin' 40s of mother earth's private nectar stock. Dodgin' cops."** I laughed. This was the craziest shit I had ever experienced. I read my first journal entry aloud several times, enjoying how it sounded. It felt like something an emcee would write. But what kind of emcee? What the hell did it mean? It was only after a few minutes that I realized what I had propped the manuscript page open with, a piece of amethyst given to me by an ex-girlfriend for my birthday. She had told me it was my birthstone and that it was known to enhance one's spiritual capacity. I had kept it on my nightstand since she had given it to me and had even held it in my hand while meditating. I picked it up and held it as I repeated those first lines over and over again. I felt strange, like I was on the cusp of something. Was it mere coincidence? I began to feel toyed with, as if somehow someone had left this manuscript specifically for me to find. The thought both frightened and excited me. The process of deciphering felt way too personal. The fact that I could only make sense of what was written after writing it in my own hand was surreal.

I spent the next six weeks copying and deciphering that one page. I would stop often to repeat the lines. They made me think of language and my experience in new and interesting ways. They inspired me to write lines of my own. I would spend whole days repeating phrases like mantras and jotting down the thoughts that came to mind as a result of them. I had been an emcee for years, but I had never written anything like this and I certainly had never heard anything like it either. I repeated it in its entirety again and again. The wordplay, imagery, and content amazed me. It spoke of the power of the spirit, of overcoming oppression, of being of an ancient lineage. It spoke directly to me. I felt empowered by it. Little doubt remained that I had come across something old and important. I would spend hours trying to figure out how something that felt so old could speak directly to these times. And, even more so, directly to me. By the time I finally finished transcribing the first manuscript page, I had it completely memorized.

On the day after I completed that first page another incident occurred. It was Friday night and I was on my way home from play rehearsal at school. I got off the subway at my regular Lafayette Avenue stop in Fort Greene, Brooklyn. I decided that I would try to find some Caribbean food before going home. I walked down Fulton Avenue in search of a veggie patty. It was about 11 P.M. and a small crowd was gathered outside of a storefront whose steamy window proved impossible to see through. A neon sign hung above the door that read "café." I opened the door and found a large group of people tightly squeezed into a small yellowish room with a woman standing before them reading a poem. A man at the door asked me if I wanted to sign up to read. It was an open mic. Immediately the manuscript page came to mind. I signed my name on the list in the last available slot. I purchased a muffin and stood near the counter next to a beautiful cinnamon-colored woman with short curly hair. She asked me if I was going to read. I asked her if she thought I looked like a poet. She looked me up and down and said, "definitely." I blushed, deep purple.

I had to sit through about ten poets before it would be my turn. I had never really sat through a poetry reading before and was amazed at the seeming popularity of this event. It was packed. The people, all young like me, would vocally respond to the images and content of the poems shared. It felt like church. The poems were mostly original, although the content matter was standard for the time: revolution. Many of the poets would read from a typed page or even from a journal. Some seemed quite shy about reading in public. By the time it was my turn I was pretty excited. The host introduced me as the final poet of the evening and I took the stage thinking, "There's no reason to be nervous. I've been on stages my entire life." I was certain I knew my "poem" by heart. I took a deep breath and began.

I had already experienced a huge surge of energy while reciting the poem to myself, but I was by no means expecting the feeling that came with reciting this poem to an audience. I could practically see the words exiting my mouth. The image of the open mouth came to mind. I was becoming the manifestation of that image. When I finished the poem there was an immense stillness. The audience seemed to have the feeling that they had just witnessed something extraordinary. They began to applaud wildly. One woman, I noticed, was crying. A man came up to me and told me that the Last Poets and Gil Scott Heron would be performing at S.O.B.'s and asked if I would like to open up for them. Another man came up and told me that Sonia Sanchez and Amiri Baraka would be reading at a Brooklyn university and asked if I would like to read at the performance as well. Another woman approached and told me that KRS One and the Fugees would be performing at Rock Against Racism in Union Square and asked if I would like to join the list of performers. I received two other invitations, one for a reading with Allen Ginsberg and another with the Roots. I had one poem. A poem that I couldn't even say that I had written. Or had I?

By this time, I had shown the manuscript to one or two friends that came over and questioned whether they were able to decipher any of the text. They hadn't, not even when I explained to them my process. Now, almost automatically I was being thrust into the world of poetry with world-renowned poets and asked to share my writing, this writing. It felt like it was bringing attention to itself. I wasn't completely comfortable with the idea, but I was even more uncomfortable with the idea of keeping it to myself. I hadn't really thought of the text as poetry. In fact, my initial thoughts were that I had come across some ancient scriptures. But then, isn't scripture very well-written poetry? I decided that I would spend more time deciphering the texts and that I would also begin to write my own words and thoughts either in reaction to the manuscript or simply inspired by my own personal journey.

I began to frequent the café, which I found out was called the Brooklyn Moon, sharing bits of the text that I had deciphered and sometimes even my own writing, and began to acquire quite a reputation. When asked about the poems I was careful to say that I could not claim authorship of the poems, although, I knew the implication was that I was taking the spiritually artistic approach of thinking of myself as a vessel. This seemed like the best explanation because there was a great deal of truth within it. I had begun to feel quite strongly that I should not reveal the origin of the writings until I had deciphered them in their entirety. With each recitation I could feel their importance growing. Often when I sat home deciphering I would slip into trance like states where I would sit for hours trying to imagine who had written them. The more I read the more I began to believe that these words had been written by someone African in origin. Perhaps some sort of shaman who foresaw slavery and the calculated oppression of African people and had planted this text to guide us through a crucial moment in our history, our future, our present. I thought intensely about the power of hip-hop. Had it, also, been planted by these African shamans as some sort of seed that would not blossom until four generations after slavery? Did it somehow hold the key to helping us express the greatest idea of freedom imaginable? Could any music have that sort of power?

Surreal, almost supernatural, things would occur every time I read aloud from the manuscript. I'd watch the words, themselves, settle into the minds of the audience and how they would leave inspired, almost as if they had witnessed something extra-terrestrial. And even within myself, the energy that would swirl within and around me as I deciphered and recited these poems is practically indescribable. But even stranger things began to happen. People began to respond as if it were their personal mission to see that these writings reach the masses. After one reading, at New York's reputable Nuyorican Poetry Café, I was approached by Marc Levin, a director, who had an idea of how these poems could work their way into a film. That film was *Slam,* which ended up winning the Grand Jury Prize at the Sundance Film Festival and the Camera D'Or at the Cannes Film Festival in France. Paul Devlin approached me and other poets from the 1996 Nuyorican Grand Slam team with plans of making a documentary of our touring experience. That film was called *Slam Nation.* One of the slam team members, Jessica Care Moore, had self-published her own book of poetry and approached me about publishing mine. That book became *The Seventh Octave,* a pre-mature collection of parts of the manuscript that I was secretly deciphering, and my own poetry, inspired by the ancient text. Next I was approached by legendary producer, Rick Rubin, who encouraged me to sign to his label, American Recordings, and record what became my first album, *Amethyst Rock Star.*

It took much longer than I would have imagined to decipher the text in its entirety. Each "poem" often left me in such a bewildered state that I could never guess what would follow. My process of deciphering remained the same, yet the text became increasingly difficult, as sometimes I would have to attempt a passage as many as thirty times before it became clear. It often seemed that I could not decipher a text until I was ready to understand it. I often took long breaks between working on the manuscript for the sake of digesting what I had already deciphered. About three years into it I began deciphering the poem entitled "Co-dead language." The long list of names baffled me. Most startling was that the writing seemed to be a direct response to the death of the hip-hop icons Notorious B.I.G. and Tupac Shakur. I had found the manuscript before either rapper had been killed, and even though I had been comfortable with the idea of this being an ancient text that had somehow fallen into my lap, when it spoke this directly to our times, I must admit, it frightened me. That fear propelled me to read it aloud as much as possible. I put it to music. I read it on TV. I couldn't listen to hip-hop the same way. I felt personally attacked whenever I felt an emcee was misusing his power. I grew angry at the way capitalism and violence was being romanticized. Then I started working on the final scroll.

I had saved the longest scroll for last. This was to be the seventh and final "poem." From the start, the tone of this page was completely different. It felt raw, unpolished, even gangster. My difficulty in deciphering it lay in the fact that I was completely surprised by the direction in which it seemed to be heading. And for a long time, I guess I wasn't ready for it. More than any of the others, I could feel its direct connection to hip-hop. The style in which it was written felt more like a rhyme than a poem. It was hardcore. So hardcore, that I abandoned it for over a year, while busying myself with other projects. Had I abandoned hip-hop too? It's true that I was listening to less hip-hop than I ever had. The growing romanticism of gangsterism and heartless pimpery had left me somewhat confused and more than a little angry. It felt like hip-hop was further off course than it had ever been. The have-nots of the African American ghettos had seemingly bought into the heartless capitalistic ideals that had originally been responsible for buying them as slaves. It felt hopeless. Hip-hop was dead. Misogyny and ignorance prevailed. Hip-hop seemed to be running the same God-forsaken course as the American government. Diamonds were as fluid as oil while the violence and corruption surrounding African diamond mines became just as overlooked as the number of dead women and children in Iraq and Afghanistan murdered in the name of American greed: the crudest oil of all. It hurt to hear emcees rapping about pointing guns at each other rather than at real enemies facing our communities and children *(, Said the Shotgun to the Head)*. It felt senseless.

Slowly my senses returned to me. Through the growing popularity of southern hip-hop, "crunk" music, "trap" music, chopped and screwed, etc., I was reminded of the original passion embedded in hip-hop music. It's not that the subject matter was any more uplifting; rather the context that shifted surrounding it. Suddenly, through hearing Southern rappers voicing their desire to once and for all "put the South on the map" I was able to see that hip-hop was still voicing a centuries old desire for respect. I was also able to realize how much of a product of America it is. This cry for respect allowed me to lose my impatience with hip-hop's overall infatuation with gangsters and realize that even that was simply a cry for power and to be recognized. Like so many, in cases when the oppressed regain a sense of power, the initial intent is to express or abuse that power in the same way that it was used against them. Men have used this sort of manipulative power over women for centuries. In hip-hop, as in America, misogyny still prevails. But that misogyny is ironically rooted in an intense and undeniable love of women. How can we uncover those roots? I slowly began to trust that I would not be shocked by my findings with this last poem. I went back to deciphering it. Sure enough, I believe that that is what the last poem (actually the first in this collection, NGH WHT) is aimed at. The problem with poetry or scripture is that even after all my deciphering, there is still much to be deciphered. Phrases must be picked apart, dissected, meditated on. There are layers of meaning.

In the bottom corner of the final page I found the last few words. What I found, I initially thought funny and quite witty. I decided to use those words for the title of the entire manuscript, *The Dead Emcee Scrolls.* Of course, it is first a reference to the ancient Judaic texts that were found in the 1940s in caves near the Dead Sea. The Dead Sea Scrolls are often confused with the Nag Hamadi, other ancient texts that were found in Egypt around the same time that claim to be, among other things, the secret teachings of Yeshua (Jesus). Both findings, along with a few others, have been of growing popularity since the pop explosion of *The Da Vinci Code,* a novel that uses factual historic data to bring light to ground-shattering truths which may have been suppressed by the early Christian church. I also believe the title to be a reference to the two hip-hop icons whose deaths have served as an example of what can happen when the power of hip-hop is misused or simply over-looked.

I have yet to fully comprehend why these texts came to me. Maybe my training as an actor, and until then, untapped talent as a writer, prepared me to write and recite them in a way that would garner the attention they now desire. I believe this release to be a part of the original author's plan. I have stopped concerning myself with the question of who wrote them and have simply found peace in knowing that "it is written." Yet, these writings have also had a profound affect on me. In fact, I will go so far as to say that they have made a poet of me. Before encountering them I had certainly dabbled with emceeing and poetry. Shit, I never lost a battle. But my rhyming and writing before encountering these texts could have easily been aligned with many a braggadocious emcee. This manuscript changed me. It forced me to decipher my own life and purpose. Subsequently, my books, *She* and , *Said the Shotgun to the Head*, were exclusively written by me. Most of the poems and songs on *Amethyst Rock Star* and the self-titled *Saul Williams* album are my own writing.

I have decided to share some of the effect that the text had on me, personally, by including some journal excerpts in the second half of this book. As I mentioned, once I encountered these texts I began to listen to hip-hop differently. I began to think differently. The journal excerpts will give you a glance into the seven years of my personal life when the majority of these texts were deciphered. They are a personal offering in light of the impersonal nature of *The Dead Emcee Scrolls*.

Through reading them you may gain insight into the way these texts helped me find my voice as a poet, emcee and artist.

Well, I guess that's it. Enjoy it. Read it to yourself or out loud to a friend. Try it over a beat. Whatever. But spend time with it. If you're an emcee, double that time and let it inform your lyricism. In many ways it probably already has. You may be surprised to see other emcees referenced either by name or by quote. Who's quoting whom? There's no explanation. Perhaps I was not the first to find this, but by some amazing grace it has found me and now I present it to you.

As for the scrolls themselves, I've kept them tucked away in hopes of one day being able to arrange some sort of exhibit. I am uncertain of the will of the "author" and, thus, have learned to sit back and allow things to unfold as they will. This has been my finding's greatest lesson to me: patience. The changes that I have wanted to see in hip-hop, American society, the black community, and the world at large, can only unfold at the rate of our evolving consciousness. People ask me why I think poetry has become popular among the youth again. I respond that we cannot achieve a new world order without new words and ways of articulating the world we'd like to experience. The youth of today are using poetry slams and open mics as a means of calling our new world into order. Hip-hop has aided our generation tremendously in helping us formulate the ability to articulate our desires and dreams over beats and in our daily lives. Word up. It is only a matter of time before we realize the importance of these times. And in the words of Victor Hugo, "There is nothing more powerful than an idea whose time has come."

SAUL WILLIAMS

I think that NGHs are the best of people that were slaves and that's how they got to be NGHs. They stole the cream of the crop from Africa and brought them over here. And God, as they say, works in mysterious ways. So He made everybody NGH, 'cause we were arguing over in Africa about the Watusi, the Baule, the Senufo . . . all in different languages. So He brought us all over here, the best, the kings, the queens, the princesses, and the princes, and put us all together and made us one tribe, NGHs.

—RICHARD PRYOR, from *Wattstax*, the film

Fellas . . . I want to give the drummer some of this funky soul we got here. You ain't got to do no soloing, brother, just keep what you got. We gonna turn it loose! 'Cause it's a Mother.

—JAMES BROWN, from "Funky Drummer"

NGH WHT

BCH NGH. Gun trigga. Dick's bigga. Why
fuck? Killer. Blood spiller. BCH stealer. Mack
truck. Bad luck, fuckin with this black buck.
Bigger Thomas, I promise. Leave a corpse in
the furnace.

NGH WHT? I'm complicated. Down to my
strut. Like the way I hold my gat, flat on its
side, like a pup. And I'm tickling the trigger.
Make it laugh from its gut. You would think
I'm a comedian the way it erupts.

NGH WHT? I represent the ashes and dust.
All the soot up in your chimney. Got you
stuck in a rut. You could fire, hold your fire,
son, I'm smoking you up. You could withhold
your desires. Even Buddha got snuffed.

NGH, now, I'm standin' on the corner of wow!
Exclamations pointed at me, 'cause I'm gattin
these nouns. Got these kids inventin adjectives.
I'm gaining renown. Because I am, NGH! I am!

NGH please. The earth, the air, the fire, and the seas. Third dimension. Fourth dimension, Fifth dimension, with ease. All that shit you never thought of. Got you smokin them trees. At your front door with my sawed-off. Got you snortin them keys.

NGH WHT? Boy I ain't gonna knock. Open up. When it's time to meet your maker, ain't no changin the plot. You're an actor in a series. NGH, I own the lot. And I'm here to serve these royalties like gold in a pot.

CHAPTER **2**

Callin haves and have-nots, every cell on the
block, every NGH with a trigga: empty barreled
or cocked. Marchin like parade of scars if you
been stabbed or shot. Son, we smokin these
batons right in front of these cops.

Callin out to the kids, all my NGHs with bids.
Whether suited up or booted up or stuck in the
mid. You can download it or boot it up. My pupils,
un-lid! All my students of the underground with
record store gigs.

Callin out to the girls. The inventors of worlds.
The intelligence of relevance and elegant pearls.
Pour like nectar from the lotus, big bang opus in
swirls, down the sweaty back of hair weave tracks
and dry Jheri curls.

Callin out to the pimps. Hat-cocked, slump, with
your gimp on your wrist with just a twist of lime
to go with that limp. Hold your cup up so this
ancient rain can find its way in. Let these NGHs
know the cost of reachin heavenly bliss.

CHAPTER 3

Here it is! The contents of a balled-up fist. All the
density of matter could never add up to this. Here's
the secret of the energy transferred by a kiss. Yes,
the secret of eternity, the secret of bliss.

And the stars: the rings of Saturn; fiery Mars; all
the jet-propelled philosophies of Venus in Furs. All
the pussy you can handle from a poet that purrs.
Chillin in a furry Kangol and some suede Timbs
with spurs.

(Arches back to hiss-story. Afternoon nap-py words.)

CHAPTER 4

Death creeps through the streets over programmed
beats. A rabid dog in heat on a dead end street. Oil
slicks: the only rainbows canvass gray concrete.
Shadows of skyscrapers fall when Mohammed speaks.

Corpses piled in heaps. Sores and decay. Reeks.
Placin tags on feet. A Nike Air Force fleet. Custom
Made: unique. Still in box: white sheet. Ripened
blue black sweet. White tank top, wife beat BREAK.

Hearts in two-step beat BREAK.
Dance pray work whip beat BREAK.
Neck back jump back kiss BREAK.

Now shake it off.

CHAPTER 5

Consider your-self: less than, inferior to,
half man, superior to, womb man, unbearable
likeness. Consider yourself: almost, never
quite, dark skinned, lily white, black as sin,
devil's den, whiteness.

Consider your-self: outcast, criminal, unseen,
invisible, point blank, ready-cocked, trigger.
Consider yourself: hardcore, dirt poor, hustler,
BCH/whore, reverend, doctor, nigger.

Cotton corn crop wheat BREAK.
Entrails tongue pig's feet BREAK.
Neck back jump back kiss BREAK.

Now break it off.

Church of: fear and lust; hell or bust; back of
bus; scream and cuss; hold your tongue; unsung
apostle. Church of: God and Christ; men and
mice; Vincent Price; naughty nice; fat suit; white
beard; colossal.

Church of: down and low; sick and shut; born
in sin; usher strut; ten percent; short on rent;
basket. Church of: Sunday suit; hex and root;
chicken foot; dusty boot; foot stomp; hand
clap; casket.

Ashes dust kill crush BREAK.
Build up pimp strut slap BREAK.
Neck back jump back kiss BREAK.
Now clap your hands to what he's doing.

Chapter 7

I came in the door. I said it before before.
The future's mistress is history's whore.
Ate the whole fuckin' apple, NGH, even the
core. Swallowed seed. Made her bleed. Now
she's begging for more.

Ancient Judaic law. Kosher, Crunk and hardcore.
Goat blood mark on the door. Open shut. Yom
Kippur. Now who's gonna take the weight? It's
your birthday. Take the cake.

Blow out the candles. I wait in the darkness,
like a vandal. The silhouette of SET in the
mirror on the mantle.

Fireplace is in the heart. Water places the art
'round the islands of desiring where most primitives
stalk, sacrificing their daughters. These primordial
waters carry a feminine agenda that no man ever
taught us.

True, they captured and caught us. Transported,
sold us, and bought us. Constituted and lawed us.
Distorted truths that they taught us. We rebelled

then they fought us. We conformed then they
formed us. Now y'all NGHs rhymin 'bout
material possessions.

False idols. False gods. Revering false titles.
Peep dude with the platinum cross. He floss
bibles. Check vitals. Revivals. Father, son in
denial. Throw momma from the train and derail
every child.

CHAPTER 8

Rape of a nation. Offbeat complete. Blood of
the Haitian. Diaspora. Divide to defeat. Euro
invasion.

Legs spread 'round midnight. "Hold still, girl.
Don't fight." Nurtured seed despite dawn's
early light.

Back to basics. Back to the streets. Jordache
and Asics. Le Tigre hoodie, fitted and neat.
Graffiti capers. The spray can vapors. Wrong
side of the track. Third rail shock treatment.
Yo I'm bringin'em back.

Unwrap the mummy. Replace his heart. Feed
him. He's hungry. Remind him of his nature.
Divine. Pictures on money. Cash in on melanin,
top of spine. He cries for mommy.

Mommy's getting raped, right now. Greco-
Roman fate, somehow. Tubman's running late,
so she plans her own escape.

She feels the music. Sign of the timeless flight
of broomsticks. Over the floor. Marital law.
The jump off movement. Movement: rhythm
and blues. Hip sways, acoustic. Wind of the
waist not want not case. Sign of improvement.

Movement: grind to unwind. The muse of
music. Even tonight, she moves despite how
dark her blues get.

Noose swings like a pendulum. Whip/crack
a/cross back, again. Simon bids his help and
then . . . DJs two worlds blend.

Feel the music. Son, we got you programmed
like a beat. When I press snare, Yo, guard your
grill. Press kick, you move your feet. You can't
compete. Got my hydrants parked on every
street. I'm federal, NGH. Son of Sun. Come
close and feel the heat.

I am the streets. The white lines only separate
me from me. You hydroplane in false god's
name and still crash into me. Sign and tree,
mountainside, guardrail into the sea. They
thought they stole you from my arms then
carried you to me.

Here's the key. DNA encoded in a beat.
White rocks in a vial, NGH, ain't got nuthin
on me. BCH, I'm free. Ask these editors at
MTV. Far as they know they're publishing
some new school poetry. Let it be. 'Cause
even that will do to turn the key. Doorways
into other worlds. The truth shall set you free.

You are me. I am you. But also I am he.
Shepherd of a bastard flock that grazes in
the streets.

Feel the beat. Nod your head. Lean back. Yo,
touch your feet. Let me see you pop that
thang right there, girl, in your seat. Feel the
heat. Count this page amongst your whitest
sheets. Comfort in my every word. Slide under.
Countless sheep.

Hail Mary, Mother of God. Got the whole
host of angels shuffling in my iPod. NGHs
learned to raise their voices when I lowered
my rod. Staff of Moses. Pharaoh knows it.
Son, my word is my bond.

Tune my heart with my mind. Speak my nature.
Divine. Called this shit into existence back in '79.
With the future in my pocket. Tightly gripped
like a nine. Keep my finger on the trigger. Waitin
for the right time.

CHAPTER **II**

Ancient NGHs align! Path of cosmic design.
Blood of kings 'cause Saturn's rings don't
need no diamonds to shine. Yes, the reason
for the season. Ornamented, divine. Coded
language of the mystics with my fist
in the sky.

Keep your head up. We represent the
real, my NGH. Dead up. Book of the
Dead. History bled. This NGH fed up.
Led us to despair, some into prayer,
and they won't let up until they got us
worshipping them false gods instead
of the realness.

God of the streets. My NGHs feel this. We
nod our heads and worship through beats.
Go 'head and kneel. It's the love that makes
the cipher complete. And it's displayed
through the way the bass line marries the beat.

Yesh, Yesh y'all. You don't stop. I spill
some liquid for my NGHs on the stop
clock. Then shake the hands of time. I
got him for his wristwatch. I got a second
wind and shook him, like in hopscotch.
Jumped the turnstile, turned, smiled, gestured:
hand crotch. Double-cross a motherfucker
'fore I get got.

Caught in the crossfire. Brought
over seas, you were caught in the
crossfire. Down on your knees,
you were caught in the crossfire.
Yeshua, please help us out of the
crossfire. The cross fire.

Caught in the crossfire. The KKK
had you caught in the crossfire.
Prayed every day, you were caught
in the crossfire. In Jesus name, you
were caught in the crossfire. The
cross fire.

Get up and walk, NGH. You the one
we was waitin for. Way before dem
Latin books bastardized the sacred law.
Made a NGH question. Mark of the beast:
deceased. Guess what's in-store? Wait for
it to register. Now, empty out that register, NGH.

And keep your hands in the sky. You the money
and the power. Get that green out your eye.
Oblivious. Hoodwinked back to black. These
NGHs wearing crosses. The shirts off their
back. Pay cash out your ass for that diamond
crack. Smoke rock-roll away or your money back.

Whipped and burned. NGH, you done
carried the cross. Made Milano a fan.
Black Madonna's the boss. You free.
Half the cost. Grace maze. Now you're lost.
Man-child in the mirror. The picture's getting
clearer and it's you.

I crossed that bridge in '72. JB played
the funky drummer. Now these fools playin
you. A lie preserved in stained glass doesn't
make it more true. Survey says, the little
drummer boy be drummin for you.

CHAPTER 14

Newborn king. Your moms: that fat lady that
sing. His eye on the sparrow. Point blank,
through a barrel. You bad to the bone. Cancer.
Sir, your marrow. I ordered the monkey. We
back to the barrel of laughs.

These NGHs God-body tryin to be golden
calves. Five percent on the corner of pure
science and math. While the eighty-five divide
their time between dead end paths. And the ten
percent have spent their rent on wars fiery wrath.

Dead Sirius. Waitin for damned self's return
to true self. True health. True school. New book
on old shelf. I, self, lord and master. Choose one
path. Move faster.

CHAPTER 15

Yeah, though I walk still talk the talk. Exorcisin
all these demons. Black board and chalk. From the
brightest constellation on land, New York. To the
origin of darkness. BREAK/POP the cork.

To all the battles fought. All the captives caught.
Lives sold and bought. Enslaved for naught.
'Cause today, we 'bout to make this freedom a
sport. Leave your jewelry in the bleachers. Come
take the court.

Yo the banana peels are carefully placed. So keep
your shell toes carefully laced. The illest NGH got
peppered and maced. Now amplify this. Turn up
the bass. And think about it.

Picture me, lampin' in the company car. Rims
like Tibetan prayer wheels. NGH WHT? I'm
a star. I cruise the block like a feather back and
forth 'til I land as the song in your ear or the
book in your hand. Now the whole fuckin world
'bout to know who I am.

Got your whole system up in my trunk. That 'dog
eat dog' make my woofers bark: atomic crunk All
my trill NGHs know who be bringin da funk. Lees
and shell toes like it's Black History Month.

Son of a vortex. African roots. That chicken foot
hex. Binary star NASA can't compute. Linear
complex. It's simple. Bloodlines span from
Lalibela temples straight to chitterling minstrels.
Spin it back to the intro.

There was one. Bore witness to the rays of the
sun. Synthesized in her own image. Photo negative.
Shun. The development of Parliament. The phallic
bop gun. Thus, the mother-ship connection spawned
the birth of the drum.

Ancient drum begat drum. Kingdom go. Kingdom
come. Ancient sector of the scepter risen up to the
sun. Hidden hand of man begat patented clone of
the drum. Boom Bap strapped into a wire, tightly
coiled, and re-spun.

Trigger sound. Trigger gun. Drum machine. Machine
gun. Bodies piled. Carefully filed under beats that were
once reprogrammed to become: unplugged concert of
sun. Every ray with sample clearance. Every two begat one.

Boom Bap hard as a gun. White cross-trainers, unstrung.
Let these suckas know the cost of making Harriet run.
Let the North Star be your guiding post when turned
from the sun until knowledge reigns supreme over
nearly everyone.

Check it out now! Check me out now!
I let these MTHRFKRs know what I'm
about now. And ain't no way no one could
ever play me out now. Because I represent
the present, NGH, right now!

Check it out now! Check me out now! At the
helm of the ship. Shipping out, now! NGH us
angel dust and devout, now! Heaven high as
the sky. Never come down!

CHAPTER 19

Attention: another dimension. Another
complicated twist too twisted to mention.
Another pair of NGH lips tongue-tied to
perfection. Another frame of mind exists
beyond comprehension.

Attention. Fourth realm of ascension.
The absence of tension. A corporate lynching.
Their god is their henchman. And he ain't
just pinching. This NGH bites! And, according
to pictures, this NGH white!

WHT?! Come down SLCTR rum pumpum
pum! Me keeps me tremor in me pocket. Come
and get some! Again! Come down SLCTR rum
pumpum pum! Me keeps me tremor in me pocket.
Come and get some!

Gimme diamond. Gimme gold. Gimme sugar.
Gimme candy. Me wine and me handy and dat
in me panty.

A stoppa! Na issa supa cat manna you a na lingo.
Tell him to come back. Tell him he a murderer. Tell
him mamma womb a she da real carrier. Woman
no a cry a you a no suffer. Tell him come a man
a who a no batter. Have mercy.

CHAPTER 20

Let me mold a guitar of your bodily bazaar.
Strap your tongue, chord your lungs, string
your toes. And bows that precede the rain
shall serpent symphonies in your name.

Mother of countless daughters. The tricks of
time. It is your thrust and grind that defines
us. We are the offspring of your decapitated
head. The bastard sons of Father Time.

Let Saturn be reborn a girl. Let her nurture
her children rather than eat them. Hide them
from our forefathers and the angry ghosts
of X-mas past. Let them be raised away from
the phallic dangers of our times.

Let their secrets remain secrets until we are
ready to cherish them as our own. Nurture
and adore them. The timeless secrets of
creation:

The darkness that yields light. The seed that
bears fruit. The mother that bears the cross
of her fathers and her fathers' fathers who

beat her when she bore no sons. His raised
fist the original Boom Bap.

Spin that record backwards. Nigger to NGH.
Before before. John the Boom Baptist. Bring
me his head. His dick. His eyes and teeth. His
arms and feet. Bring me all that is mine, all that
has been buried, scattered or lost until history
is ours again.

Mothers of night and windsong. Daughters of dust
and detriment. Nameless. Fuck it. Let them remain
nameless. It won't stop their truth from prevailing.
Because it is not written. Because it don't matter
anyway. Because there's nothing you can do about
it. Because there's no excuse, no explanation.
And that is reason enough to

Dance. Even when your feet hurt.
Dance like the fires of hell are upon
you and you're dodging every flame.

Dance when it tastes good.
Dance when the spirit moves you.

Dance because you feel it and you don't
have to be taught how to count, how to step
and slide, how to twirl and jump and land
on a good foot before taking off to fly,

NGH, dance. Dance, nigger. Paint your faces.
Shine your shoes. Pop that collar. Shake it.
Wind it. Kick fight scratch rip kill BREAK.

Neck back jump back kiss BREAK.
Uprock freeze pop lock BREAK.
Don't stop don't stop snap BREAK.

Into ferocious song and dance. Calculated
movement. Gestures of prayer and invocation.
Dance. Your life depends on it.

Cakewalk. Lindy. Charleston Mashed potatoes.
Camel walk. Hot pants. Hustle. Electric boogaloo.
Patty Duke. Steve Martin. Pee-wee Herman.
Prep. Wop. Rooftop. Cabbage Patch. Chicken
head. Ragtop. Wobble. Crump. Snake. BREAK!

You wish you could dance like this! You wish!
Standin there. High postin. You wish. "And our
American Idol is Fantasia."

"You know you want me, Mickey. You
can't afford me, though. My name is Saturn,
Pluto. I ain't no Disney ho."

Sing it, girl. Sing it. Southern trees bear
strange WHT?! Sometimes I feel like a
motherless WHT?! Drop beats like bombs

in Alabama churches, Afghani libraries,
New Jersey turnpike, the sphinx's nose,
crack in Compton, AIDS in Africa, small
pox in blankets, blue-eyed Jesus, the Holy
Ghost and all dem other covered women,
fallen soldiers and noblemen.

Mother turned whore turn in graves
turn to each other and help us over-
turn tables.

Turntables. Nails sharp as needles.
Vaseline on faces. Scratch scratch
scratch scratch.

BREAK BREAK

Scratch scratch
scratch scratch.

BREAK BREAK

Kick kick snare.

BREAK

Scratch kick snare.

BREAK

Snare kick, kick. Kick, snare. Snare
kick. Snare. Snare kick, kick, kick,
kick, kick, kick kick, snare.

Snare kick, kick. Kick, snare. Snare
kick. Snare. Snare kick, kick, kick,
kick, kick, kick kick, snare.

Snare kick, kick. Kick, snare. Snare
kick. Snare. Snare kick, kick, kick,
kick, kick, kick kick, snare.

Snare kick, kick. Kick, snare. Snare
kick. Snare. Snare kick, kick, kick,
kick, kick, kick kick, snare.

Chop and screw it.

BREAK it down beneath labyrinthine
corridors of anguish and despair. The
chamber the bullet travels. Chamber of
commerce. Tunnel vision of the train
over tracks . . .

Not until you listen to RKM on a rocky
mountaintop have you heard hip-hop.
Extract the urban element that created it
and let an open wide countryside illustrate it.

Riding on a freight train in the freezing
rain listening to Coltrane. My reality went
insane and I think I saw Jesus. He was
playing hopscotch with Betty Carter who
was cursing out in a scat like gibberish for
not saying butterfingers.

And my fingers run through grains of sand
like seeds of time. The pains of man.
The frames of mind which built these frames
which is the structure of our urban super-
structure.

The trains and planes could corrupt and
obstruct your planes of thought so that
you forget how to walk through the woods
which ain't good 'cause if you never
walked through the trees listening to Nobody
Beats The Biz then you ain't never heard
hip-hop.

And you don't stop. And you don't stop.
And you must stop letting cities define you.
Confine you to that which is brick and cement.
We are not a hard people. Our domes have
been crowned with the likes of steeples.

That which is our being soars with the eagles
and the Jonathan Livingston Seagulls. Yes, I
got wings. You got wings. All God's children
got wings. So let's widen the circumference
of our nest and escape this urban incubator.

The wind plays the world like an instrument.
Blows through trees like flutes. But trees won't
grow in cement. And as heart beats bring
percussion fallen trees bring repercussions.
Cities play upon our souls like broken drums.

We drum the essence of creation from city
slums. But city slums mute our drums and
our drums become humdrum 'cause city slums
have never been where our drums were from.

Just the place where our daughters and sons
become offbeat heartbeats.

Slaves to city streets. Where hearts get broken
when heartbeats stop. Broken heartbeats become
break-beats for NGHs to rhyme on top.

CHAPTER 24

I'm falling up flights of stairs. Scraping
myself from the sidewalk. Jumping from
rivers to bridges. Drowning in pure air.

Hip-hop is lying on the side of the road
half dead to itself. Blood scrawled over its
mangled flesh like jazz. Stuffed into an over-
sized record bag.

Tuba lips swollen beyond recognition. Diamond
studded teeth strewn like rice at karma's wedding.
The ring bearer bore bad news. Minister of
Information wrote the wrong proclamation. Now
everyone's singing the wrong song.

Dissonant chords find necks like nooses. That
NGH kicked the chair from under my feet.
Harlem Shaking from a rope, but still on beat.
Damn that loop is tight! NGH found a way to
sample the way, the truth, the light. Can't wait to
play myself at the party tonight. NGHs are gonna
die!

Cop car swerves to the side of the road. Hip-hop takes its last breath. The cop scrawls vernacular manslaughter onto his yellow pad, then balls the paper into his hands, deciding he'd rather freestyle.

You have the right to remain silent. You have the right to remain silent. You have the right to remain silent. And maybe you should have before your bullshit manifested.

CHAPTER 25

Begin. Demystify the mummy within. If you
ain't hotep then ho step, I'll step to your friend.
Parable of the wind. Blew black through to the
end. Endless nights, kicks and fights against time
and her friends.

Slowly day and night blend. Twilight takes form
and then open sky sprouts an eye: solo, singular,
sin. Downward glance, upward grin. Half the
women are men. Children born of the morn grow
until daylight's end.

Sunset sets on the wind. Blue-black blows once
again. Ever since ever after henceforth happy ending.
Children born of the wind take the night as their
friend. Starlit sky, many-eyed wonder of the within.
Fear: original sin. Death: nowhere near the end. Once
upon break o'dawn's early Lyte: Paper Thin.

CHAPTER **26**

When you say you love me a series of changes
begin to occur. First there is a warmth. The warmth
generates heat. The heat permeates the cold. The ice
melts. Limbs and branches are thawed. Blood
circulates. A feeling of comfort pervades.

The body is oxygenated. It becomes limber. It yearns
to dance, to move about freely and express its newfound
energy. Music is sought through voice or ear. The heart
identifies the rhythm of the song and synchronizes its
pace. A union is formed between the visible and the
invisible.

Song is the invitation from the primordial unseen to
become one with that which is seen. To nod your head
is to agree that the moment is godly: communion. To
dance is to become God. There are many ways of dancing.
Follow your heart.

CHAPTER 27

A circle forms. I enter. Footsteps from side to
side. I am forming figure eights with my feet.
Footwork, centuries old, reconfigured for the
present. NGH WHT: the expression on my face,
the name of the faceless. One hand on the ground,
then the other. Baby swipes. Legwork. Knee spin.
I'm nice with this shit. Hand spin into windmill
into head spin: Revolution. Here and now, NGH.
Who's next?

CHAPTER 28

In a past life I was a wood-carver's knife. The
sharpened blade of a woodcutter. The eldest
son of the chief's brother. A maker of drums.

We scraped the insides of goat hides to find
the hollows where sound resides. Offering
the parts we did not use. To invoke the muse.

Music of the ghettos, the cosmos, the negroes,
the necros: overcomers of death; disciples of
breath. Dissection of drumbeats like Osiris
by Seth.

Breakbeats into fourteen pieces. Dissembled
chaos. Organized noise. A patchwork of
heartbeats to resurrect true b-boys. Be men.

Let's mend the broken heart of Isis. Age of
Aquarius. Mother Nature is furious. While
you rhyme about being hardcore, be heart-
core. What is it that we do art for?

Metaphor. Meta-sin. It's an age of healing.
Why not rhyme about what you're feeling?
Or not be felt. Deal with the cards you're
dealt.

Calling all tarot readers and sparrow feeders
to cancel the apocalypse. Metaphorically
speaking.

The corner coroner. I smoke for weeks. Dead Pan,
like dead man, through chimney peaks. I streak the
skyline. I blew through bird. High notes. I space
float. I'm lost for words.

The storefront preacher. The Sunday best. The
dangling cross between legs, on chest. The country
farmer. The hoedown champ. The rhythmic armor.
The cosmic dance.

The buck and gully. The native son. Bigger and Deffer.
The freshest one. The sewed-in creases. The flavored
twills. The confidence snorted through dollar bills.

The "Fuck I care for?" The boldfaced lie. The been
there and done that. The do or die. The dirty dirty.
The filthy clean. Thugged out and nerdy. No in
between. The blackest berry. The sweetest juice.
That complex NGH born of simple truth.

The solar/polar. The chosen side. The black face
mammy of the bluest eye. The battered woman.
The dream deferred. Now caught up and paid in
full, that's my word.

The jungle brother. The sly and stone. Rock hard,
NGH. Give a dog a bone. The marrow's morrow.
The newest breed. The headline merger between
word and deed.

The search for balance. The quest for peace. A
tribe called NGH. NGH WHT, the chief. The
distant lover. The close-up clown. The iced-out
grill with the screw-face frown.

A wealth of violence. A violent wealth. You caught
up, NGH, better watch your health, the beat is dope
though. The junkie nod. The use of breakbeats to
beat the odds.

The odds are even. I paper rocks. Rocks smash
scissors. NGHs trigger Glocks. The blackened
target. The dick-long chain. NGHs kill NGHS
in Jesus' name.

God and pussy. Objects of desire and ill repute.
Some'd rather seek up high, than dig and grind
that inner truth. The angel of my eye a bit too fly
to substitute with any other form than the messiah's.

Black Maria, mother ship, grandmother moon
and sea. The wave and form of beauty born
of Eden's apple tree. And every single atom
stands erect and prays to be the follower she
offers sweet communion.

Holy union. Let me see you wind it, just like
that. Move your hips from side to side. Come
forward, push it back. Let me know firsthand
the land of glory that I lack. I surrender all to
you if you'll surrender back.

Holy crap. Where'd you learn to squeeze it
tight and then move it slow enough for me
to question everything? You slowly start to
tremble. Heaven's walls begin to sing.

Tsunami ever after. Cosmic slop on everything.

CHAPTER 31

Shower me with blessings. No second-guessing.
'Cause God, herself, is sitting on the edge of my
bed, slowly undressing. A night symbolic as the
resurrection. I'm about to slide up in the kingdom
of God with no protection.

And I can guarantee a second coming. 'Cause I
already hear the drummer boy barumpumpum
pumming. A host of angels look at me through
your eyes. My first communion with my hands
on your thighs. You're catching the spirit, the Holy
Ghost and the fire. Yo, this is wild.

I'm every Jay-Z album played in reverse. I'm
risen from blunt ash and stashed in a purse.
I'm smuggled over borders, contraband, 'though
I rock. I paper. I scissor. Nah, NGH, no Glock.

I'm the aftermath of five percent you figure
aftermath. One hundred twenty lessons cover
one-third of my path. Two totes of what I spoke
contents hit and system crash. The greenery of
scenery, but essence dark as hash.

Pay me cash. Simply 'cause what money means
to you. Your currency has currently devalued
what is true. When freedom rings through costly
bling, it's overdrawn, past due. The bankroll of
an empty soul kept vaulted. Code and clues:

NGH WHT, I represent the truth you claim to be.
The hero of the eastern sky, the storm's eye, westerly.
Rough, rugged, raw, eternal law recited over beats.
Some poetry to oversee the dance floor and the streets.

Feel the beat. Understand the rhythm that you seek.
Let it be your guiding force you speak from when
you speak. Hold your tongue just long enough to
find your path, unique. Then spit the seeds the forest
needs to garner what we reap.

It ain't deep. As simple as a breakbeat and some
rhymes. Type of shit to nod your head while
chillin with your dime. But hold her tight, 'cause
she just might read deep between the lines and start
to think the words that she now reads are simply mine.

Give them voice. Spit them over beats. Repeat. Rejoice.
An anthem you can put in your own words or chant.
Your choice. May heaven smile upon your earthly reign
b-girls and boys, as it has upon mine: fancy pens on paper,
poised.

It's divine. Every page a different sort of kiss. No, not
for everyone. This pen is clenched in a black fist. And if
that ain't your cup of tea, perhaps, a glass of piss. So hold
your nose and drink it down. Just think of it as Crys-.

But if it is, if you don't mind the source from whence
I speak, and recognize you can't disguise the source of
every beat, then nod your head, girl, wind that waist,
bend over, touch your feet. And go ahead and pop that
thang. Yes, yes, cipher complete.

AMETHYST
ROCKS

CHAPTER **I**

I stand on the corner of the block slinging
amethyst rocks. Drinkin 40's of mother
earth's private nectar stock. Dodgin cops.
'Cause Five-O be the 666 and I need a fix
of that purple rain. The type of shit that
drives membranes insane. Oh yeah, I'm in
the fast lane. Snorting candy yams. That free
my body and soul and send me like Shazaam!

Never question who I am. God knows.
And I know God, personally. In fact, he
lets me call him me. I be one with rain
and stars and things, with dancing feet
and watermelon wings. I bring the
sunshine and the moon. And wind blows
my tune.

Meanwhile I spoon powdered drumbeats
into plastic, bags. Sellin kilos of kente scag
Takin drags off of collards and cornbread
Free-basin through saxophones and flutes
like mad. The high notes make me space
float. I be exhalin in rings that circle Saturn.
Leavin stains in my veins in astrological patterns.

Yeah, I'm Sirius B. Dogon NGHs plotted
shit, lovely. But the feds are also plotting
me. They're trying to imprison my astrology.
Put my stars behind bars. My stars in stripes.
Using blood-splattered banners as nationalist
kites. But I control the wind. That's why they
call it the hawk.

CHAPTER 3

I am Horus. Son of Isis. Son of Osiris.
Worshipped as Jesus. Resurrected like
Lazarus. But you can call me Lazzie. Lazy.
Yeah, I'm lazy 'cause I'd rather sit and build
than work and plow a field of cash green crops.

Your evolution stopped with the evolution
of your technology. A society of automatic
tellers and money machines. NGH WHT?
My culture is lima beans. Dreams manifest.
Dreams real. Not consistent with rational.

I dance for no reason. For reason you
can't dance. Caught in the inactiveness
of intellectualized circumstance. You
can't learn my steps until you unlearn
your thoughts. Spirit/soul can't be store
bought. Fuck thought. It leads to naught.
Simply stated, it leads to you trying to
figure me out.

CHAPTER 4

Your intellect is disfiguring your soul.
Your being's not whole. Check your flagpole:
stars and stripes. Your astrology's imprisoned
by your concept of white, of self. What's your
plan for spiritual health? Calling reality unreal.
Your line of thought is tangled.

The star-spangled got your soul mangled.
Your being's angled, forbidding you to be real
and feel. You can't find truth with an ax or a
drill, in a white house on a hill, or in factories
or plants made of steel.

CHAPTER 5

Stealing me was the smartest thing you ever
did. Too bad you don't teach the truth to your
kids. My influence on you is the reflection you
see when you look into your minstrel mirror
and talk about your culture.

Your existence is that of a schizophrenic vulture
who thinks he has enough life in him to prey on
the dead, not knowing that the dead ain't dead and
that he ain't got enough spirituality to know how
to pray. Yeah, there's no repentance. You're bound
to live an infinite, consecutive, executive life sentence.

So while you're busy serving time, I'll be in synch
with the moon, while you run from the sun. Life of
the womb reflected by guns. Worshipper of moons,
I am the sun. And I am public enemy number one.
One. One. One. One. One. One. That's seven. And
I'll be out on the block. Hustlin culture. Slingin
amethyst rocks.

UNTIMELY
MEDITATIONS

Time is money. Money is time.
So, I keep seven o'clock in the
bank and gain interest in the
hour of God. I'm saving to buy
my freedom. God grant me wings.
I'm too fly not to fly. Eye sore
to look at humans without wings.
So, I soar. And find tickle in the
feather of my wings. Flying
hysterically over land. Numerically,
I am seven mountains higher than
the valley of death, seven dimensions
deeper than dimensions of breath.

The fiery sun of my passions
evaporates the love lakes of my
soul, clouds my thoughts and
rains you into existence. As I take
flights on bolts of lightning.
Claiming chaos as my concubine
and you as my me. I of the storm.
You of the sea. We of the moon.
Land of the free. What have I done
to deserve this? Am I happy?

CHAPTER 3

Happiness is a mediocre standard
for a middle-class existence. I see
through smiles and smell truth in
the distance. Beyond one dimensional
smiles and laughter lies the hereafter.
Where tears echo laughter.

You'd have to do math to divide a
smile by a tear, times fear, equals
mere truth, that simply dwells in the
air. But if that's the case all I have
to do is breath and all else will follow.
That's why drums are hollow.

And I like drums. Drums are good.
But I can't think straight. I lack the
attention span to meditate. My attention
spans galaxies. Here and now are immense.
Seconds are secular. Moments are mine.
Self is illusion. Music's divine.

CHAPTER 4

Noosed by the strings of Jimi's guitar,
I swing, purple-hazed pendulum. Hypnotizing
the part of eye that never dies. Look into my:
eyes are the windows of the soul is fried chicken,
collards, and cornbread is corn meal, sour cream,
eggs, and oil is the stolen blood of the earth, used
to make cars run and kill the fish.

Who me? I play scales. The scales of
dead fish of oil-slicked seas. My sister
blows wind through the hollows of fallen
trees. And we are the echoes of eternity.
Maybe you've heard of us.
We do rebirths, revolts, and resurrections.

We threw basement parties in pyramids.
I left my tag on the wall. The beats would
echo off the stone and solidify into the
form of lightbulbs, destined to light up
the heads of future generations. They
recently lit up in the form of: BA BOOM
BOOM OM. Maybe you've heard of us.

CHAPTER 5

If not then you must be trying to hear us
and in such cases we cannot be heard. We
remain in the darkness, unseen. In the center
of unpeeled bananas, we exist. Uncolored by
perception. Clothed to the naked eye. Five
senses cannot sense the fact of our existence.
And that's the only fact. In fact, there are no
facts.

Fax me a fact and I'll telegram a hologram
or telephone the son of man and tell him he
is done. Leave a message on his answering
machine telling him there are none. God and
I are one. Times moon. Times star. Times sun.
The factor is me. You remember me.

I slung amethyst rocks on Saturn blocks
until I got caught up by earthling cops. They
wanted me for their army or whatever. Picture
me: I swirl like the wind. Tempting tomorrow
to be today. Tiptoeing the fine line between
everything and everything else. I am simply
Saturn swirling sevens through sooth. The sole
living heir of air. And I (inhale) and (exhale) and
all else follows. Reverberating the space inside of
drum hollows. Packaged in bottles and shipped to
tomorrow, then sold to the highest NGH.

I swing from the tallest tree. Lynched by
the lowest branches of me. Praying that
my physical will set me free 'cause I'm
afraid that all else is vanity. Mere language
is profanity. I'd rather hum. Or have my
soul tattooed to my tongue. And let the
scriptures be sung in gibberish. 'Cause
words be simple fish in my soulquarium.
And intellect can't swim.

So, I stopped combing my mind so my
thoughts could lock. I'm tired of trying
to understand. Perceptions are mangled,
matted, and knotted anyway. Life is more
than what meets the eye and I.

So, elevate eye to the third. But even that
shit seems absurd when your thoughts
leave you third eye-solated. No man is an
island. But I often feel alone. So find peace
through OM.

OM

Through meditation I program my heart
to beat break beats and hum bass lines
on exhalation. BA BOOM BOOM OM.

I burn seven-day candles that melt into
12-inch circles on my mantle and spin
funk like myrrh. BA BOOM BOOM OM.

And I can fade worlds in and out with my
mixing patterns. Letting the earth spin as I
blend in Saturn. NGHs be like spinning
windmills, braiding hair, locking, popping,
as the sonic force of the soul keeps the planets
rockin.

The beat don't stop when soul-less matter
flows into the cosmos trying to be stars.
The beat don't stop when earth sends out
satellites to spy on Saturnites and control
Mars.

'Cause NGHs got a peace treaty with Martians
and we be keepin'em up to date through sacred
gibberish like "Sho Nuff" and "It's on." The
beat goes on. The beat goes on. The beat goes
OM. BA BOOM BOOM OM.

And I roam through the streets of downtown
Venus tryin' to auction off monuments of Osiris'
severed penis. But they don't want no penis in
Venus, for androgynous cosmology sets their
spirits free.

And they neither men nor women be. But they be
down with a billion NGHs who have yet to see that
interplanetary truth is androgynous.

And they be sendin us shout outs through shootin
stars. And NGHs be like, "what up?" and talking
Mars. 'Cause we are solar and regardless of how
far we roam from home the universe remains our
center, like OM. BA BOOM BOOM OM.

CHAPTER 3

I am no earthling. I drink moonshine on Mars
and mistake meteors for stars 'cause I can't hold
my liquor. But I can hold my breath and ascend
like wind to the black hole and play galaxophones
on the fire escape of your soul.

Blowing tunes through lunar wombs. Impregnating
stars. Giving birth to suns that darken the skins that
skin our drums. And we be beatin infinity over sacred
hums. Spinning funk, like myrrh, until Jesus comes.

And Jesus comes every time we drum. And the moon
drips blood and eclipses the sun. And out of darkness
comes the BA BOOM BOOM. And out of darkness
comes the BA BOOM BOOM. And out of darkness
comes the BA BOOM BOOM OM.

1987

Acid wash Guess with the leather patches,
sportin the white Diadoras with the hoodie
that matches. I'm wearing two Swatches and
a small Gucci pouch. I could have worn the
Louis but I left it in the house.

My NGHs Duce and Wayne got gold plates
with their name, with the skyline on it and the
box-link chain. I'm wearing my frames they
match my gear with their tint. And you know
Lagerfeld is the scent.

My NGH Rafael just got his jeep out the shop.
Mint green sidekick. Custom made ragtop. *Strictly
Business* is the album that we play. "You're a
Customer," the pick of the day.

There's a NGH on the block. Never seen him
before. Selling incense and oils. My man thinks
that he's the law. But why on earth would this be
on their agenda as he slowly approaches the window.

Uh, uh, I've seen you before. I've been you and
more. I was the one bearing the pitcher of water. I
rent the large upper room furnished with tidings of
your doom or pleasure, whichever feathers decree.

"Yo, Ralph, is he talking to me?" "No I'm talking to
the sea sons resurrected. I'm the solstice of the
day. I bring news from the blues of the Caspian"

My man laughs. "He's one of them crazy
MTHRFKRs. Turn the music back up. 'Cause
I'm the E double." "Wait, but but, I know the
volume of the sea and sound waves as I will.
Will you allow me to be at your service?"

My man Ralph is nervous. He believes his
strange tongue deceives and maybe he's
been informed that he's pushing gats, Hidden
in the back beneath the floor mats. "Come on

Jack, we don't have time for your bullshit or
playin, As Salaam A somethin or another."
"Wait isn't Juanita your mother? I told you
I know you. Now grant me a moment."

CHAPTER 3

"At the gates of Atlantis we stand. Ours is the blood that flowed from the palms of his. Hands on the plow, till earth 'til I'm now. Moon cycles revisited. Womb fruit of the sun. Full moon of occasion wave the wolves where they run. And we run towards the light. Casting love on the wind. As is the science of the aroma of sleeping women."

Lost in his eyes. They soon reflect my friends are grinning. But I'm a pupil of his sight. The wheels are spinning. "Yo, I'll see y'all later tonight."

CHAPTER 4

In the beginning her tears were the long awaited rains of a parched Somali village. Red dusted children danced shadows in the newfound mounds of mascara that eclipsed her face, reflected in the smogged glass of Carlos' East Street bodega.

Learning to love she had forgotten to cry, seldom hearing the distant thunder in her lover's ambivalent sighs. He was not honest. She was not sure. A great grandfather had sacrificed the family's clarity for gold in the late 1800s. Nonetheless, she had allowed him to mispronounce her name, which had eventually led to her misinterpreting her own dreams and later doubting them. But the night was young.

She, the first-born daughter of water, faced darkness and smiled. Took mystery as her lover and raised light as her child. Man that shit was wild. You should have seen how they ran. She woke up in an alley with a gun

in her hand. Tupac in lotus form, Ennis' blood
on his hands.

She woke up on a vessel, the land behind her,
the sun within her, water beneath her, mushed
corn for dinner. Or was it breakfast? Her stomach
turned, as if a compass. She prayed east and lay
there breathless. They threw her overboard for
dead. She swam silently and fled into the blue Si.

CHAPTER 5

La So Fa Me Re Do Si. The seventh octave. I
don't mean to confuse you. Many of us have
been taught to sing and so we practice scales.
Many of us were born singing and thus were
born with scales.

Myrrh-maids cooks and field hands sang a
night song by the forest and the ocean was the
chorus in Atlantis, where they sang. Those thrown
overboard had overheard the mysteries of the
undertow and understood that down below there
would be no more chains.

They surrendered breath and name and survived
countless as rain. I'm the weather, man. The clouds
say storm is coming. A white buffalo was born
already running. And if you listen close you'll hear
a humming.

CHAPTER 6

Beneath the surface of our purpose lies rumor of
ancient rain. Dressed in cloud-face, minstrels the
sky. The moon's my mammy. The storm holds
my eye.

Dressed in westerlies. Robed by Robeson. Ol'
Man River knows my name. And the reason you
were born is the reason that I came.

CHAPTER 7

Then she looks me in the face and her eyes get
weak. Pulse rate descends. Hearts rate increase.
Emcees look me in the face and their eyes get
weak. Pulse rate descends. Hearts rate increase.

Emcees look me in the face and their eyes get
weak. Pulse rate descends. Hearts rate increase.
It's like "Beam me up, Scottie." I control your
body. I'm as deadly as AIDS when it's time to
rock a party.

We all rocked fades. Fresh faded in La Di Da Di.
And when we rock the mic we rock the mic right.
But left's the feminine side. Ignored the feminine
side.

I presented my feminine side with flowers. She cut
the stems and placed them gently down my throat.
And these tu lips might soon eclipse your brightest
hopes.

SHA CLACK CLACK

CHAPTER I

I could recite the grass on a hill and memorize
the moon. I know the cloud forms of love by
heart and have brought tears to the eye of a
storm. My memory banks vaults of autumn
forests and Amazon River banks. I've screamed
them into sunsets that echo in earthquakes.
Shadows have been my spotlight as I monologue
the night and dialogue with days. Soliloquies of
wind and breeze applauded by sunrays.

We put language in zoos to observe caged
thought and tossed peanuts and P-Funk at
intellect. And MTHRFKRs think these are
metaphors. I speak what I see. All words
and worlds are metaphors of me. My life
is authored by the moon. Footprints written
in soil. The fountain pen of Martian men
novelling human toil.

And, yes, the soil speaks highly of me, when
earth seeds root me poet-tree. And we forest
forever through recitation.

Now maybe I'm too Sirius. Too little here
to matter. Although I'm riddled with the
reason of the sun. A standup comet with the
audience of lungs. This body of laughter is
it with me or at me? Hue more or less? Hu-
man, though gender's mute. And the punch-
line has this lifeline at its root.

I'm a star. This life's the suburbs. I commute.
Make daily runs between the sun and earthly
loot. And raise my children to the height of
light and truth.

CHAPTER **3**

If I could find the spot where truth echoes,
I would stand there and whisper memories
of my children's future. I would let their
future dwell in my past so that I might live
a brighter now.

Now is the essence of my domain and it
contains all that was and will be. And I
am as I was and will be, because I am and
always will be that NGH. I am that NGH.
I am that NGH.

I am that timeless NGH that swings on
pendulums like vines through mines of
booby-trapped minds that are enslaved
by time. I am the life that supersedes
lifetimes, I am.

It was me with serpentine hair and a timeless
stare that with a mortal glare turned mortal
fear into stone time capsules. They still exist
as the walking dead. As I do, the original
suffer-head, symbol of life and matriarchy's
severed head: Medusa, I am.

It was me, the ecclesiastical one, that pointed
out that there was nothing new under the sun.
And in times of laughter and times of tears, saw
that no times were real times, 'cause all times
were fear. The wise seer, Solomon, I am.

It was me with tattered clothes that made you
scatter as you shuffled past me on the street.
Yes, you shuffled past me on the street as I
stood there conversing with wind blown spirits.
And I fear it's your loss that you didn't stop

and talk to me. I could have told you your future as I explained your present, but instead, I'm the homeless schizophrenic that you resent for being aimless. The in-tuned nameless, I am.

CHAPTER 5

I am that NGH. I am that NGH. I am
that NGH. I am a negro. Yes, negro
from necro, meaning death. I overcame
it so they named me after it. And I be
spitting at death from behind and putting
"kick me" signs on its back, because,

I am not the son of Sha Clack Clack. I
am before that. I am before. I am before
before. Before death is eternity. After death
is eternity. There is no death there's only
eternity. And I be ridin on the wings of
eternity, like yah, yah, Sha Clack Clack.

I exist like spitfire which you call the sun,
try to map out your future with sundials. But
tic toc technology can no tic toc me. I exist
somewhere between tic and toc. Dodging it like
double-dutch. Got me living double-time. I was
here before your time. And my heart is made of
the quartz crystals that you be making clocks out
of. And I be resurrectin every third, like tic tic
Sha Clack Clack.

No, I won't work a nine to five, 'cause
I'm setting suns and orange moons and
my existence is this . . . still, yet ever moving.
And I'm moving beyond time. Because time
binds me it can set me free and I'll fly when
the clock strikes me, like yah, yah, Sha Clack
Clack.

But my flight doesn't go undisturbed, because time makes dreams defer. And all of my time fears are turning my days into daymares. And I live daymares, reliving nightmares, that once haunted my past. Sha Clack Clack. Time is beating my ass.

And I be havin nightmares of chocolate-covered watermelons filled with fried chicken, like piñatas, with little pickaninny sons and daughters standing up under them with big sticks and aluminum foil, hitting them, trying to catch pieces of falling fried chicken wings.

And Aunt Jemima and Uncle Ben are standing in the corners with rifles pointed at the heads of the little children. Don't shoot the children! I shout. Don't shoot the children! But it's too late. They start shooting at the children and killing them one by one, two by two, three by three, four by four, five by five, six by six . . .

but my spirit is growing seven by seven. Faster than the speed of light, because light only penetrates the darkness that's already there. And I'm already there. I'm here at the end of the road, which is the beginning of the road beyond time, but where my NGHS at?

CO–DEAD
LANGUAGE

Whereas, break-beats have been the
missing link connecting the diasporic
community to its drum-woven past.

Whereas, the quantized drum has
allowed the whirling mathematicians
to calculate the ever-changing distance
between rock and stardom.

Whereas, the velocity of spinning vinyl,
Cross-faded, spun backwards, and re-released
at the same given moment of recorded history,
yet, at a different moment in time's continuum
has allowed history to catch up with the present.

We do hereby declare reality unkempt
by the changing standards of dialogue.

Statements such as, "keep it real," especially
when punctuating or articulating modes of
ultra-violence inflicted psychologically or
physically or depicting an unchanging rule
of events, will henceforth be seen as retroactive
and not representative of the individually
determined IS.

Furthermore, as determined by the collective consciousness of this state of being and the lessened distance between thought patterns and their secular manifestations, the role of men as listening receptacles is to be increased by a number no less than 70 percent of the current enlisted as vocal aggressors.

MTHRFCKRs better realize, now is the time to self-actualize. We have found evidence that Hip-hop's standard 85 RPM when increased by a number at least half the rate of the standard or decreased by 3/4's of its speed may be a determining factor in heightening consciousness. Studies show that when a given norm is changed in the face of the unchanging the remaining contradictions will parallel the truth.

Equate rhyme with reason. Sun with season. Our cyclical relationship to phenomena has encouraged scholars to erase the centers of periods thus symbolizing the non-linear character of cause and effect.

Reject mediocrity. Your current frequencies of understanding outweigh that which has been given for you to understand. The current standard is the equivalent of an adolescent restricted to the diet of an infant. The rapidly

changing body would acquire dysfunctional
and deformative symptoms and could not properly
mature on a diet of applesauce and crushed pears.

Light years are interchangeable with years of living
in darkness. The role of darkness is not to be seen
as or equated with ignorance but with the unknown
and the mysteries of the unseen.

Thus, in the name of: Robeson,
God's son, Hurston, Akhenaton,
Hatshepsut, Blackfoot, Helen,
Lennon, Kahlo, Kali, The Three
Marias, Tara, Lilith, Lourde,
Whitman, Baldwin, Ginsberg,
Kaufman, Lumumba, Gandhi,
Gibran, Shabazz, Shabazz,
Siddhartha, Medusa, Guevara,
Gurdjieff, Rand, Wright, Banneker,
Tubman, Hamer, Holiday, Davis,
Coltrane, Morrison, Joplin, Du Bois,
Clarke, Shakespeare, Rachmaninoff,
Ellington, Carter, Gaye, Hathaway,
Hendrix, Kuti, Dickerson, Ripperton,
Mary, Isis, Theresa, Plath, Rumi,
Fellini, Michaux, Nostradamus,
Neferttiti, La Rock, Shiva, Ganesha,
Yemaja, Oshun, Obatala, Ogun,
Kennedy, King, four little girls,

Hiroshima, Nagasaki, Keller, Biko,
Perón, Marley, Shakur, Those who
burned. Those still aflame. And the
countless un-named.

We claim the present as the pre-sent as the
hereafter. We are unraveling our navels so
that we may ingest the sun. We are not afraid
of the darkness. We trust that the moon shall
guide us. We are determining the future at this
very moment. We now know that the heart is
the philosopher's stone.

Our music is our alchemy. We stand as the
manifested equivalent of three buckets of water
and a handful of minerals, thus, realizing that
those very buckets turned upside down supply
the percussive factor of forever. If you must
count to keep the beat then count. Find your
mantra and awaken your subconscious. Carve
your circles counter-clockwise. Use your cipher
to decipher coded language, man-made laws. Climb
waterfalls and trees. Commune with nature snakes
and bees.

Let your children name themselves and claim
themselves as the new day for today we are
determined to be the channelers of these

changing frequencies into songs, paintings,
writings, dance, drama, photography, carpentry,
crafts, love, and love.

We enlist every instrument: acoustic, electronic,
every so-called race, gender, sexual preference
every per-son as beings of sound to acknowledge
their responsibility to uplift the consciousness
of the entire fucking world!

Any utterance un-aimed will be disclaimed,
will be maimed. Two rappers slain!

Seven poems. Seven glimpses into an unknown mind with hints and insights into our own. What is a poem but a means of making sense of all that comes through the senses, a senseless dream decoded? What is a dream but a story broken into fragments and scattered, card-like, before a child as a test of memory? What is memory but a warm welcome from a stranger who knows you by name and perhaps a kiss and invitation to board in a larger room with greater storage space and more natural light? But there are also memories that haunt, past moments that we'd rather think of as belonging to past lives. And then there are those stored in books and records for the sake of collective memory: history.

The history of the African American population is a page torn from precolonial African history books and pasted into the scrapbooks of the New World. Enslaved Africans were the original record of a people sampled, chopped, screwed, looped, noosed and used as the repeated hook of a national anthem: a hit record. When a people are cut off from their language, their culture, their religion and traditions they are forced to adopt, adapt and forge new ground over old wounds. Much has been said about the dangers of stripping people from their roots. What we seldom hear is the story of those born naturally into societies that are steeped in age-old traditions that have felt unable to find or pursue their individual paths because the ideologies of their culture have not evolved at the same rate as them. In this sense, traditions can subjugate and restrict the rate of the growth of a people. In some cases, when a people are freed from their past they are given an opportunity to start anew. Hip-hop, like its African American creators, is born of this newfound independence. It is our generation's opportunity to start from scratch.

Hip-hop is a revisionists' draft of history. It is a state of mind that refutes all states but its own. In the early days of music videos, Run DMC stood defiantly outside of the Rock and Roll Hall of Fame claiming to be the Kings of Rock, without singing and without a band: a statement and gesture as audacious as sticking a national flag on the moon. Their stance typifies the stance of hip-hop. It is a stance that takes and samples elements of its own history and dares to slow it down, speed it up or do whatever is necessary for it to fit into a new conception of the present. It is harder drums added to a popular jazz riff, a guitar solo spun backward and released in even increments over a high-powered kick drum. It is the angry snare of a lion that has been trapped, a final warning before attack. Hip-hop is the most aggressive stance that any people has ever taken at how one can and should relate to his or her history. It samples the past, while at the same time, re-ordering it and declassifying its hidden roots. It is the voice of the newly emancipated as they begin the process of being able to clearly state and declare their independence.

But what if the voice of independence misaligns itself with ideals and values that bespeak more so of enslavement than independence? What if the youth are misguided into believing that money is the ultimate power or that vulnerability is weakness? How does a newfound voice of independence avoid the pitfalls of its predecessors? And what ultimately is the cost, look, and feel of freedom? Can it be bought? African American slaves who bought their freedom still had to avoid interacting with the elements of society that would not acknowledge the papers that certified them as free. There are countless stories of freed men or women simply having their certificates of freedom torn up and finding themselves chained and carried back into slavery. Their money and ability to purchase anything, including property or freedom, was not enough to over-rule the prevailing mentality of the times. Are these not the truths that withstand time? What will it take for a people that served at the lowest rung of capitalist hierarchy to not buy into the mentality that originally bought them as slaves? At what point does the power of hip-hop begin to work against itself? At what point does hip-hop reflect more of its American birthplace than its African roots?

The power of the spoken word is very much a part of the power of hip-hop. The emcee stands in direct lineage to the African griot. The African griot/story-teller plays a major part in the history of spoken art forms and the oral traditions of poetry. A tradition that has a much longer and more widespread history than that of the written word. The sport of spoken word, as relates to modern phenomena, such as slam poetry, is not a newfound in-terest, rather it is a return to ancient rites and gatherings that have been known to have occurred for thousands of years. Ancient poets such as Kabir, Rumi, Hafiz, and even the Greek Homer were known, in their time, for the recitation of their work. Thus, the young poets of today are part of an ancient tradition that is perhaps the eldest in creative expression. The spoken word move-ment in connection to hip-hop has become a place where the youth have stripped away the beat of the drum to simply focus and sharpen the attention paid to the word. Listening to young poets read in a poetry slam, you are bound to hear them recite their own coming of age stories, which may often be inclusive of the story of their parents, grandparents, or ancestors. Through the simple act of reciting their poem they are adding their voice to the telling of his/story, which was once linear and exclusive of them and the particularities of their story, their perspective. These new poems allow us new insights into the past, which then allows us a broader conception of the present and grants us the ability to re-envision the future. Simply stated, it changes everything.

Most emcees are also concerned about telling their own coming of age stories. Their voices are easily likened to the voices of young poets, often contemplative and introspective to the point of questioning their reality, upbringing, and the society that bore them. Yet, where a special form of attention is paid to crafting a poem or a prayer, it is seldom the same sort of attention used in writing a rhyme. The braggadocio aspects of emceeing are a distinguishing factor. Part of the unique power of hip-hop is its internal sense of competition. Every emcee is automatically pitted against the others. The competitive nature of the art helps create an environment where most are concerned about displaying their skills while at the same time putting down the skills or abilities of others. As in any gladiator-like sport, those involved are most concerned about not leaving themselves vulnerable on any given side. It is this factor that serves to distinguish the emcee from the poet. Whereas an emcee may see displaying his or her vulnerabilities as a weakness, a poet will often see the ability to display vulnerability as a strength. It is when the careful balance between the two is found that hip-hop is at its most powerful.

My experience with these texts has been life-changing, to say the least. I have discovered that there are distinct experiences to be had through reading or reciting them. For instance, the experience of reading the words NGH WHT, spelled with no vowels, as was commonly practiced in spelling the name of God (YHWH) or gods in the written forms of ancient Hebrew and Kemetic languages (KMT is the original name of ancient Egypt), is quite distinct from hearing the commonly used "nigga" or "nigger." It takes a step further the idea of a term once used to degrade now being used as a term of endearment. In fact, the document brings to question whether it is actually asserting that NGH WHT is the name of God (absurd, I know, but it definitely seems to imply so).

The rhythm of these seven poems is also of great interest. Whether read aloud or to oneself the rhyme patterns are easily decipherable, quite often complex, and seem to cover many distinct styles of emceeing. The complexity of the rhyme patterns of certain chapters seems to correlate to the complexity of the subject matter. Yet, the content of a recited piece, even of great complexity, is much more easily digestible through the use of rhyme and rhythmic patterns.

It has been a great temptation of mine either to footnote or to write a complete companion piece to these seven poems. Yet, I believe that there is more insight to be found by sharing it with as many as possible and allowing people to discover their own references and viewpoints. My opinions on the text and on hip-hop are my own. I can claim no true authority over the art form or the varied voices of our generation. I am one of many. It has been my intention to share these words in their written form for the sake of accomplishing what I have believed to be my personal responsibility since finding them. Regardless of how they reach you, one thing remains clear: Whether hip-hop is the offspring of the streets or a seed planted by ancient African shamans whose foresight allowed them to plant seeds in the hearts and minds of a stolen people, only to blossom four generations after slavery for the sake of expressing the highest ideas of freedom, it's ours, or in the words of T-La Rock, it's yours.

PART 2

SEVEN MOUNTAINS:

JOURNAL EXCERPTS 1994–2001

1994

These are, perhaps, some of the greatest moments of my life. I have "been led" or "fallen into" or "happened upon" a series of events, revelations, insights that have brought on some of the most intense feelings and experiences I have ever had. My overall search has been effortful, but these newly acquired insights, sensibilities, and thoughts have been effortless steps toward a greater state of awareness. These past few days I have had several awkward or mystical occurrences, which were almost immediately confirmed as "real" or "valid" in a later moment.

I have been led to adopt new beliefs, which seem to be a prerequisite to existing beyond the mirror. I am very sure that there is much to be experienced beyond the mirrors of this physical realm. By "beyond" I mean seeing past an image or through, within, or behind it. Yet, also seeing it as it is. And I mean "is" in the fullest sense. I am both blessed and burdened. Now that I know, or am at the beginning of knowing, I must act or be eternally un . . .

∞

I was born today.

Just now.
Just now.
Just now.

Just now.
Just now.

∞

Mixed emotion
Contrived commotion
Natural struggle
Lead-filled sacks
On non-burdened backs
Finding the time to love
In the midst of chaos
It birthed us, nourishes us
We live in it and for it
If we were free
We'd fight for the freedom
To recreate it.

Who's your master?
Your dreams of disaster
Nightmares of freedom
Fantasies of fantasies
Which you claim we have no time for
Because we're being choked?
Well, what if time ceased to be time?
How would that affect your tomorrows of freedom?
Where would that leave us, today?
Would you then find the time to inhale and exhale
And wear those hands around your neck

As a necklace, accessorizing your
Newfound suit of

Mixed emotion
Contrived commotion . . .
. . . infinity

∞

How can I escape this cycle?
Must I turn with the world
In the direction it dictates?
Am I the wind's slave?

∞

As instruments come to life with breath
The wind sends my high notes
To indigo communions
With Coltrane's *Favorite Things*

This is my body, which is given for you
This is my blood which is shed for you

My love, like the wind, uncaged,
Blows time into timeless whirlpools
Transfiguring fear and all of its subordinates
(possession, fear, jealousy)
into crumbling dried leaves

My love is the winds slave
and, thus, is free

my love is the wind that is shaped
as it passes through the lips of earthly vessels
becoming words of wisdom
songs of freedom or simply hot air

my love is the wind's song:
if it is up to me, I'll never die
if it is up to me, I'll die tomorrow
one thousand times in an hour
and live seven minutes later.
If it's up to me, the sun will never
Cease to shine and the moon will
Never cease to glow
And I'll dance a million tomorrows
In the sun rays of the moon waves
And bathe in the yesterdays
Of days to come
ignoring all of my afterthoughts
And pre-conceived notions.
If it is up to me, it is up to me.
And, thus, is my love
Untainted, eternal.

The wind is the moon's imagination
wandering.
It seeps through cracks, explores the unknown,
Ripples the grass.

My love is my soul's imagination.
How do I love thee?
Imagine

∞

And will I now forget everything that I have read? Will I not now attempt to actualize the glimpses of a higher reality that I have experienced? What did Siddhartha teach me? And Azaro? And all of the other spirit children? And the insights? Have they not all laid the groundwork for this new de/con/struction of self?

I have learned the importance of stories, the importance of dreams (night and day), the need to look beyond mirrors, the flow of energy, the hindrances of "control dramas," the inconsistencies of time, the inaction that self-consciousness leads to, the reality of the "unreal," the universal source of energy, the beauty of all things, the unity of all things, that coincidences aren't, that love cannot be specified (kinda), the ineptitude of belief, death only comes to those who believe in it, life only comes when you're not reading, writing, or thinking about it. "Life is what happens when you're busy making other plans."

∞

I could inhale your existence
And exhale your dreams
And this room would be filled
With things that only seem
Your mind's on permanent rewind
Trying to make it fast forward

Press record, listen,
Beyond what you hear
Pre-occupation with time
Is pre-occupation with fear

"Looking at my Gucci it's about that time"
the tick tock of clocks padlock your mind

capital centered on your left wrist
your reality is twisted, unreal

capital is not center
time is undefined
as soon as you define it it's a new time
but with unchanging minds
new times become same times
why blame time for bad times or sad times
sometimes I forget time
and exist on my own time
I own time
The concept exists in my own mind
And mind is eternal
That concept defeats time
So I climb . . .

African - American
Drumbeat - For money

∞

Where I live
Music notes take the form
Of dollar signs
Souls sing backup
While material desires
Sing solo

∞

Somewhere between self-hate and Brooklyn
I sit on a mountain of green-leafed questions
Searching for balance in the mist
I used to rock beats over lunch room tables
Now I'm searching for balance in the midst

And I find bliss in mental tugs of "what for?"
'cause they make me think I'm deep
Raising dead questions like a grammatical visionary
Who can only see the past in the future

Come one come all
I can make the blind walk

"And I run through discotheques like sound."

Figuring I'm bound to hear something
That I can nod my head to
But everything is "For the killers
And the Hundred Dollar-Billers"
And "Real Niggas who ain't got no feelings"

I got mad feelings
And stay broke

Too broke to buy a magnum
Or a state of mind
To help my thoughts go platinum

∞

I was discovered by Gold
Mined and marketed as meat
Erased of my memories
So I'd have the freedom to think
I discovered that which discovered me
And then made it my God, mistakenly

∞

I take shots of molasses
So I can slow my existence
And feel the world
Spinning on its axis

I want to feel revolution
For myself
Fuck the Franz Fanon books on the shelf
I mean, really,
I just want to dance
'cause I remember when
We used to back spin and windmill
Breakbeats wouldn't let niggas stand still
We'd feel the music
Begin to swipe and spin
'til we were dizzy
From revolution
On the dance floor

∞

They call dancing primitive.
They call singing senseless.

Some have forgotten to hum.

They are too busy with the
"how to" and "why."

My culture will never die.
It lives in the wind.

". . . and the very rocks will cry out."

Skyscrapers will fall
Your lack of understanding
Will crush you down to "primitive."

Maybe all of us.

∞

We all travel the same road. Alone.

∞

Blinded by the brightness of darkness, I stepped forward into a world where shadows precede breath. I could feel all of my pores opening to the point of being enveloped by openness: a black whole. Being entered by the many colors of darkness, the bows that precede the rain, as humid as the center of a raindrop, I began to orbit my new realm. There was no looking back.

I had no eyes. But language dictated that I saw. I was all eyes just as I was all else. Surrounded by a darkness that held the unmuted intensity of every color in its shadow. We were one and millions.

My name. Somebody was calling my name. I saw no one. Then I realized that that which I was hearing as my name wasn't, but was the sound of unmuted colors gathered in the wind, swirling against time. The sound of bright resonant darkness. The sound of orphan shadows rejoicing in the light. And that was my name. It was all of our names. And I, too, joined in the calling.

∞

I perform biopsies
On cyclopses
So that I might better understand
My third eye

Dissecting words
May be clever
But I aim to live verbs

To be

∞

Calculating the distance
From here to forever
The square root of me is circular
But such calculations
Are a waste of time
And pre-occupation with time
Is a waste of life
But what am I
Supposed to do
With this calculator?

Too many caged birds
Sing of dreams deferred
Too few chance beyond
The Maya of these hues

∞

Siblings of soil
Soiled and shunned
Gather your seeds
A garden of guns
Armored archaic
Garnished by sun
Guiltlessly growing
A garden of guns
Petalled with passion
Tended by nuns
Target tomorrow
A garden of guns

∞

An un-aimed bullet
Shot in a storm
Maimed the magician's
Rabbit as he performed
In his dream. In his dreams

He seldom fails. He knows
The magic of the close-eyed
Angels who cast spells on
The nightfall's descent.
This night was like no other.
All dreams were aimed and blunt.
All children saw the rabbits appear
Out of nothing.

The void of the magicians hat.

∞

Sitting on the steps
Of wood creeks and song
Dust blown and driven
By journeys too long
Ancient decrepit spiders of space
Eight-legged infinity
Webbed wisdoms brown face

Capital trades slave
Manhood's maroon
Captive of conscience
Freedoms' buffoon

Maybe at noon
Maybe right now
Never to know
Ancient as sound

Highest vibrations
Unheard untraced
Ghetto's Gibran
Sneakers unlaced

∞

I am a powerless vessel. A reed of the wind. One of many. There is no genius of my own. Speak through me.

Now, why do wish to be spoken through? Is it so I can receive credit for that which comes through me? If that's the case then I am not ready to be spoken through. Not until it is learned that there is no credit for me to bathe my vanities. I would taint the cleansing waters. Not until I lose all sight of audience for my sake should I have audience for your righteousness never to be forsaken.

∞

I am simply attempting to master the art of losing myself in everything in which I can invest myself

Self evacuation procedures to follow in case of ego:

∞

Yes, the black gold of the sun
Father of Saturn
Descendent of Run
Spoonie not Biggie
Ill beats and bass
You know my case number

1,2,3,4,5,6,7
Father reverend
Mother star
Carlos gypsy
These all who I are
Stars of the sky
In relation to the eye
Third child
Of the mind of Duce
Sketched on the drawstrings
Of a noose
The descendent
Of ill beats and choruses
The llamas be Michaels
The scarabs be Horus'

∞

And if I could Van Gogh these vanities
So that I may display artistically
The hell where I dwell, egotistically
Yo, I'd transcend physically
And become the sun
To make picturesque
This souls arson

Son, you'll never shine
Until you find your moon
To bring your wolf to a howl
So fetch your cows and spoons

∞

It doesn't matter
What I say anymore
I am the solstice of a union
U and I verse the world
And I have the power
To bring rain from the sun
And radiance from the moon
Blessed be the womb

∞

Complex theories
To discover simplicity
Abstracted illusions
The problem with chemistry is biology
The problem with biology is physics
The problem with science is metaphysics

Killed by your theories of death . . .

1997

Prisons be like magnets
Attracting delinquent habits
Maybe that's why niggas
Steel wheels spinning
To counter the attraction
Spray my name on steel horses
To loosen the reins

Cry the eyes of a thousand storms
Galloping o'er the clouds
Chariots of the morn
Foot soldiers of the wind
Handmaidens of the dawn

The archers are aimed at the unnamed
The rain-bows and arrows
Truth is bloodstained
Yet, Brutus is an honorable man
'Though he has Caesar's blood on his hands
And he claims that his palms are bleeding
But no doves grace the sky of his eyes
And the sun still must set in the west.

By no means the darkest ray of the sun
A shaman of shadows

Cast your net in my lungs
And reap the dreams of my breath
Of these hymns seldom sung
Black's the gift
To be young
To be young

Dreams deferred
So Ray-sinned in the sun

I sold clouds in a rainless season
Nickel bags, dimes of rhyme and reason

As if clouds were treason
The warden storms
Through wintered cells
Avalanched rhetoric
Me and reason rebel
My mind's consciousness in a snowsuit
My third eye strapped in ski boots
They crucified their Lord on snowboards
The iceman cometh
Plug the sun in
A hundred Miles' trumpets
And runnin
With the music
Loop the drumbeat
Tambourine gone?
Shake your shackles

I'm handcuffed to the sample machine
Shoot the sheriff and throw me the key

Bull's eye
Blood shot
Matadors of the wind
I'm charged
With possession of illegal substance

But my substance
Makes eagles of the ill

∞

1987?

A story of self-remembering. Season and Claire are connected through many past-life experiences. The old man who approaches Season in the beginning of the poem is Season as an old man. So, Season as a young boy meets Season as an old man, and slowly young Season makes the connection.

Claire (short for Clairvoyance): her great grandfather sacrificed the family's clarity for gold in the late 1800s.

They are each other's eternal reflection: reflection eternal.

It is the story of a vortex that opened in 1987 and its effect on 2 people. The story of 2 people who begin to remember their past lives and their relation to history and the future in order to prepare the world for its oncoming destruction/evolution: the rains.

∞

They stood and waited on the seafloor. It had been written that their number would be two score and nine. Dead man float. The living found new life three miles beneath the boat.

He had been drowning for a day or two. He could no longer see the sky he left behind when he looked from whence he fell. He floated in the face of darkness, never noting when that face became his own. He knew the city, still below him, was his birthplace. He held his breath with dreams of living a million deaths from home. He had been told that he would see its sky beneath him, yet he saw no clouds. He took note of the clouded forms through which he drifted. The sleeping woman had been the first. Her resonant purr had been the birth of earthquakes. She floated alone in the darkness . . .

He drifted deeper.

The faint sound of a drum could be heard.

The city stood in shades of blue, gated by the dreams of those living high above in a world inhabited by those who never knew of the ones that swam beneath them.

He stood facing the wall of dreams, deciphering the master key from the mystery.

∞

She took from the ocean
With wings of water
Sea-feathers flapped weather
Waved worlds blue girls . . .

∞

And soon the dungeons
Became crystal caves
Where light prisms
Un-prisoned slaves
And we basked in our own reflections
And sought new ways to channel
Our light

∞

A child is born in the ghetto
Only three toes
And a finger nailed
To crosses street to
Avoid trouble
Carries cowries in his knapsack
And a book of things to come
Keeps his soul inside his sneaker
Ties his laces with his tongue

∞

Now I know niggas with triggas
Cocked and ready go gettas
My man got dimed and did time
And all my sons on the shine

Yo son, I got the answer
Lack of melanin is cancer
Melatonin when you're home and alone
Your cover's blown

Classified and unknown
Yo, what's the password?
My old man's last words labeled as absurd
But my spirit knew

"Yes, the peel ripens to black
But we aim for the blue"

We, the sea sons of Atlantis
Grace the night with our hue. . . .

∞

I am closer to where I want to be than I ever have been and experience more internal doubt than I ever have.

∞

I think I should aim at nothing more than ridding myself of lying, negative attitudes, trying to control how people see me, overconcern about what others think of me, dishonest expression of emotions, trying to possess that which isn't mine, false humility, lack of discipline: physically, mentally, spiritually and of all that leaves me incapable of giving and receiving love.

Simply, I don't have to try to be a poet or how I imagine a poet should or would be. I don't even have to write, as long as I am honest to each moment rather than to my ideas of myself.

∞

I had black coral around my neck
So I could only see the sea
Its salted water in my eyes
Parade as tears

The dancing girls
March down my cheeks
Twirling my fears

But the band
Plays on and on
Despite the years

Every morning
I rise and face
The firing squad
Every morning
There is one
Who holds his fire

His dilemma
Is my system of belief

They fire rounds
But I am seldom
In their circle
A quiet mind
Is labeled "sound"
And colored purple

My little girl
Has not yet learned
To color within lines
Her jumbled diction
Has not yet learned
Our contradiction
We speak of art

With flaming passion
Then do work
Void of compassion
And wonder why reality
Is bleeding fiction

∞

Nigga, you better drink
Half a gallon of Shaolin
Before you pluck the strings
Of my violin

My life is orchestrated
Like London symphony
Concentrated
Niggas waited and waited
I'm birthday wishes, belated

∞

I write in red ink
That turns blue
When the book closes

∞

In 1972
My mother was rushed
From a James Brown concert
In order to give birth to me

My style is black whole
Most niggas simply sound like earth to me

If hip-hop were the moon
I'd be the first to bleed
Cyclical sacraments of self
For all my peers to read

I recite the hues of night
With spots of light
For you to read by

Have you floating
On cloud nine
Without realizing
It's mind's sky

And the ground
On which you walk
Is the tongue
With which I talk

I speak the seeds
That root the trees
Of suburbia New York
City streets

Could never claim me
That's why I never sound like you

All these niggas
Claim the streets
As if paths through the woods
Ain't true

You better walk your path
You better do your math
'Cause your screw face
Will only make the Buddha laugh

Even if you know your lessons
You don't know the half
But don't take it from me
Son, take a bath

∞

I was walking down Fifth Avenue today when Russell Simmons came out of a building and crossed right in front of me.

Is that the same as a black cat?

∞

They are preparing
To introduce me
To their god
I will simply ask him
Whether he'd like to join
Our entourage

"Show him to his room!"

Let him rest
For we rise early
And no god
Is gold enough
To tempt the darkness
From these mines

∞

The universe gives us every opportunity, lays the perfect path of obstacles, that through overcoming them we will have achieved the perfect balance and thus achieve the ultimate alchemical mixture of the God composite.

∞

Dear God,

I wasn't breast-fed and most of my conversations with men seem to revolve around music. I'm no musician, but the pain has been instrumental. My senses: finely tuned instruments of being lonely, of being loved, of being hue man. I'm no musician, but my life seems to be orchestrated by the likes of women.

∞

Leading a new lover
To the dance floor

Is like taking your intended
To meet your parents
You hope everything works out
That there is no miscommunication

1999

Cancel the apocalypse!

Cartons of the Milky Way with pictures of a missing planet last seen in pursuit of an American dream. This fool actually thinks he could drive his Hummer on the moon, blasting DMX off the soundtrack of a *South Park* cartoon. Niggas used to buy their families out of slavery. Now we buy chains and links, smokes and drinks. And they're paying me to record this. Even more if you hear it. Somebody tell me what I should do with the money? Yes, dread, tell me what you think I should do with the money. Exactly how much is it gonna cost to free Mumia? What's he gonna do with his freedom? Talk on the radio? Radio programming is just that, a brain washed and cleaned of purpose. To be honest, some freedom of speech makes me nervous. And you, looking for another martyr in the form of a man, hair like a mane, with an outstretched hand . . . in a world of harsh thoughts, reactionary defensiveness and counter-intelligence, what exactly is innocence? Fuck it. I do believe in police brutality. Who do I make checks payable to? How about I pay you in prayers.

A young child stares at a glowing screen, transfixed by tales of violence. His teenage father tells him that that's life, not that Barney shit. A purple dinosaur who speaks of love. A black man who speaks of blood. Which one is keeping it real, son? Who manufactured your steel, son? Hardcore, based on elements at the earth's core. Fuck it, I'm gonna keep speaking 'til my throat's sore.

An emcee tells a crowd of hundreds to keep their hands in the air. An armed robber steps into a bank and tells everyone to put their hands in the air. A Christian minister gives a benediction while the congregation holds their hands in the air. I love the image of the happy Buddha with his hands in the air. Hands up if you're confused. Define tomorrow. Your belief system ain't louder than my car system. This nigga walks down my block with a rottweiler, a sub-woofer, on a leash. Each one teach one. A DJ spins a new philosophy into a barren mind. I can't front on it. My head's as if to clean the last image from an Etch A Sketch. Somethin' like Rakim said. I could quote any emcee, but why should I? How would it benefit me? Karmic repercussions. Are your tales of reality worth their sonic-based discussions?

Suddenly the ground shivers and quakes. A newborn startles and wakes. Her mother rushes to her bedside and holds her to her breast. Milk of sustenance heals and nourishes. From the depths of creation, life still flourishes. Yet, we focus on death and destruction, violence and corruption. My people, let Pharaoh go!

What have you bought into? How much will it cost to buy you out? How much will it cost to buy you out of the mentality that originally bought you, a dime a dozen? Y'all niggas are a dime a dozen.

∞

Puffy's in the boardroom.
I'm in my room, bored.

Your success made me doubt myself
And the whirling ways of this world.

∞

Man, this love of hip-hop is like investing in a marital relation-ship, way past its prime, simply for the sake of the children, not realizing that we are actually fucking up their entire conception of relationships. They will be forced to work it out for the rest of their lives, falling in and out of love.

I've outgrown you.

I enjoy my memories of you much more than I enjoy our present moments. You allowed yourself to be defined by some-thing less than yourself. But then, I never really stopped loving you. In fact, I love you more and began to love you through your manifestations in others: a breakbeat in a Led Zeppelin song; braggadocio in a Guns n' Roses song; a breakbeat sped up to twice its speed in a drum and bass song. In my estimation, Portishead is hip-hop. Tricky is hip-hop. Björk is hip-hop. And they are hip-hop in ways that you have failed to be. Perhaps, they are hip-hop's illegitimate children.

If hip-hop is a parent, it is negligent, not nurturing, and hardly responsible. But I can blame no one but myself. I ex-pected too much of you without making my own contribution. I quit rhyming at the age of seventeen. Maybe my quitting on hip-hop led to hip-hop quitting on me.

Regardless, y'all have succeeded in making my earliest in-spiration hardly an art form, hardly the voice of the youth anymore. You guys are boring, predictable. And maybe that's why I'm working with Rick Rubin now. This is part of his karma.

∞

Brown bags on the corner
Pants cuffed at his shin
Keloid from a razor
Right under his chin
Son's looking at me
No sign of recognition
Sun shines on my left
No time for superstition

I peep the bulge in his vest
The smell of the.çess
The glare of distress
The fear of the rest
The mark of a test

The mark of the beast
The streets of the east
The laws of the west
The flaws of the west
The cause of this mess

The haves and have-nots
The gets who get got
The shots from the cops
And cops who get shot
Innocents getting popped
Got whole blocks down on lock

But son's looking at me
Yo why you looking at me?

I turn around and look back
Look down and look back
Say a prayer and look back
Yo, why you looking at me?

∞

I wake up with doubt and fear. The first two faces I see in the morning, first cousins of the face of death (which I later found out was only a mask). The first thing I smell is most usually hesitation.

This feels like the kind of slump that is only healed by tragedy . . . or is that me willing something into existence?

I'd rather be propelled than go by foot.

I want her to call me first. At least that way I can construct a window in this house of fear.

A cardboard box called home.

These are the thoughts of the sinking. My pen man ship is the Titanic.

Maybe I've idolized too many dead geniuses. They all wore the same costume to the masquerade party hereafter.

Maintain a safe distance from these ideas. They are simply the many i's attempting to be your capital. "I" that is.

These ideas float around my head like many little islands around the globe.

I may write something brilliant that I may not be able to read due to poor pen man ship.

See what I mean? That one was smaller than Tahiti.

A volcanic land mass.

Like an open wound.

∞

I bowed to her
And when I rose
Found my head
In my hands

I bore a gift
Yet at the same time
Bore the pain

∞

He was pronounced dead.
Pronounced dead.
Is that all it takes?

∞

I was born at 12:30 in the morning. By 1 AM I was certain I would not remember much of my past. By 1:40 I had forgotten my name. By 2:12 the ancients had bid me farewell. By 2:30 I had swallowed a foreign brand. By 2:40 I had begun to hallucinate. It's all coming back to me. I met my parents' spirit guides at 4:30. It was they who told me of the sun. It was not what I expected. It only seemed to hint at light.

By 6:17 I had decided what I wanted to be. At 6:18 I discovered my outer shell. At 6:19 I began the process of dying: piss, shit, and crying, crawling and not flying. At 7 o'clock my mother held me and rocked. The spinning world stopped. She sang, "You're the one. Indivisible son of sun, ancient mystical spirit come to become our tongue. . . ."

∞

As the rockets' red
Glare in your eyes
Will you look down
Or glare back

As the one
Who defies?

∞

I am concerned about a repetition of events. History only re-
peats itself for those who do not know their history. I must
learn to accept each situation as a (k)new (unknown) situation,
regardless of how much it appears to be a repetition of things
that once occurred (yet, with different characters).

New—Knew
Knew—New

I love English. Through its dissection a million things are
under/over-stood.

∞

This is a new day.
Believe it or not.
Re-live it or not.

∞

Everyday I am led
Into another room
Of your mansion

How foolish I must sound
Complaining about how wet
God's kisses are

Mental states
Have physical boundaries

∞

How could you not
Realize the power of word
After being forced
To serve a sentence?

∞

The walking dead
Walking with their own
Solar systems of blood and tissue
Circling around them

We are coming forth by day
And swollen with sway

∞

Once upon a dawn's early light
The symbols assembled
Crosses of every sort
Emblems of every fort
Phallic and lunar
Mystic and solar

Symbols of civilizations past
Politics and heretics
Of the asterisk
Mathematic symbols
At the cusp of a new age
Gathered on the grains
Of a brown page

I am not a writer
I am the plight
Of unfigured equations:
A stick of cinnamon
A grove a cloves
Cayenne and a bowl of honey
Water and money

$$\infty$$

And the irony of the evening
Was that only the white DJ
Would spin the record
With the refrain
"Black man know yourself.
Don't forget your past."

We cannot forget
Our past because
You will re member it
For us

Collective consciousness

∞

Will there be war
Declared on this soil
In my lifetime?

History tells me, yes.
But I have difficulty
Imagining fighting
Something that ain't
Invisible.

∞

Can music change the world?
Are these simply songs to be heard
And forgotten?
When JB said, "Say it loud . . ."
Did that affect a shift in consciousness?
Can the music of a society
Help mold its mental state?
Can a great song affect more than the way
A musician approaches his next song?
How about the way they approach their children.
Their loved ones, their lives?

I believe that I am
A man molded by music

And my intent is to mold
To shape
These are the ways
Of a carpenter

∞

What has become
Of my simple truths?

They have become
Complex lies.

∞

You close your eyes
When the beat swells
Feathers in inkwells
My word is bird
Purple pigeon
Of a street tale
Learned the ropes
Like strange fruit
Cloaked in brown shells
My tongue, the noose
Of untruth
Chants, prayers, and spells

∞

Delegate of the
Unconventional

Member of the
Society-less

Author of the
In between

The graffiti on the
Whitewashed wall
Of the institution,
Now crumbled,
Has become
The cornerstone
Of our compound

Compounded dreams
Distilled vessels, refilled
Belief systems
Will be billed
Payable to
Who you pray to

If you wish
To pay in person
Addresses may vary
According to beliefs

Some will have to die first

Some may have to suffer
And be free from desires

Some may have to purge themselves,
Fast, cover their heads, think less
Of women, beat their children, abstain
From the secular world . . .

Yet others may simply be
Themselves
And in being and embracing
All aspects of the mother:
Patience, responsibility,
Compassion, open-heartedness
They will find themselves
Provided for, they will find
Their dreams fulfilled, they
Will find their spirits nurtured,
And their hearts healed

∞

Wind washed wonderful
Whirlwinds through water
Welcome to the New World
Where words wind and shadow
Whither and whistle worship

The weather call to the clouds
Walk through the winter
A week of new sounds
We wish for clear water
It's a wonder her wing-fruit
Seeds smile like my daughter
Whether she will or
Whether she won't
The wind will still whistle
Through thistles and thorns

∞

Son of the Sun
Friend of the wind
Life of the womb
Reborn once again

∞

May the sun shine through
Your clouded testament

∞

Silent angel
Wingless words
Women who dance
Meaning into shapes
Shapes that are symbols
Of truths to come

The past tense of drum
Is dream

We dance through
Memories, unseen

We are dancing women
The subconscious
Of our ancestors
The contents of feathers
And webs, rewoven
The fabric of a future
Once fable

The legend
Of a legion
Of angels

∞

The only metaphor that
Exists is midwifery
All else is sight specific
Most things are
Hardly more than they are

There is midwifery in poetry
Midwifery in dance

The artistic process is
A process of midwifery

If we do not catch
These falling stars
Then we will experience
No more than a cratered
Wilderness but when truth
And beauty falls into our hands
And we learn how to place it back
Into the arms of the mother . . .

You finish the thought

∞

The depths of breath
Is all that is left
To breathe shallow
Is to wallow in doubt

Here on the darkened wood
Of this misshapen tree
There is no trace of age
Its rings have been stained
And tarnished
There is no telling
Of ancestry or lineage

It no longer matters
We are here now
Conjurers of the evermore

I cannot invest in these surroundings
For only I am held accountable
And the wages of unwritten pages
Is shallow breath

It is only through this
That we might replant
These forests

Libraries are forests
Replanted. . . .

∞

That which I was born
I am no longer

That which I was born
I have lived well beyond

That which I was born
Yet I am

As an artist
First, I was black.
I wrote with a yearning
To be a leader. I was
Born into a mourning
Race. We mourned
The death of a king.
I awoke to find
My tongue a scepter.

2001

Inner breathlessness, outer restlessness
By the time I caught up to freedom I was out of breath
Grandma asked me what I'm running for
I guess I'm out for the same thing the sun is sunning for
What mothers birth their young'uns for
And some say Jesus' coming for
For all I know the earth is spinning slow
Sun's at half-mast 'cause masses ain't aglow
On bended knee, prostrate before an altered tree
I've made the forest suit me
Tables and chairs
Papers and prayers
Matter vs. spirit

A metal ladder
A wooden cross
A plastic bottle of water
A mandala encased in glass
A spirit encased in flesh
Sound from shaped hollows
The thickest of mucus released from heightened passion
A man that cries in his sleep
A truth that has gone out of fashion
A mode of expression

A paint-splattered wall
A carton of cigarettes
A bouquet of corpses
A dying forest
A nurtured garden
A privatized prison
A candle with a broken wick
A puddle that reflects the sun
A piece of paper with my name on it

I'm surrounded
I surrender

All
All that I am I have been
All I have been has been a long time coming
I am becoming all that I am

The spittle that surrounds the mouthpiece of the flute
Unheard, yet felt
A gathered wetness
A quiet moisture
Sound trapped in a bubble
Released into wind

Wind fellows and land merchants
We are history's detergent
Water soluble, light particles,

Articles of cleansing breath
Articles amending death
These words are not tools of communication
They are shards of metal
Dropped from eight-story windows
They are waterfalls and gas leaks
Aged thoughts rolled in tobacco leaf
The tools of a trade
Barbers barred, barred of barters
Catch phrases and misunderstandings
But they are not what I feel when I am alone
Surrounded by everything and nothing
And there isn't a word or phrase to be caught
A verse to be recited
A mantra to fill my being

In those moments
I am blankness, the contained center of an "O"
The pyramidic containment of an "A"
I stand in the middle of all that I have learned
All that I have memorized
All that I've known by heart
Unable to reach any of it
There is no sadness
There is no bliss
It is a forgotten memory
A memorable escape route
Only is found by not looking

There, in the spine of the dictionary
Words are worthless
They are a mere weight
Pressing against my thoughtlessness
But then, who else can speak of thoughtlessness
With such confidence
Who else has learned to sling these ancient ideas
Like dead rats held by their tails
So as not to infect this newly-oiled skin

I can think of nothing heavier than an airplane
I can think of no greater conglomerate of steel and metal
I can think of nothing less likely to fly
There are no wings more weighted
I too have felt heaviness
The stare of man guessing at my being
Yes I am homeless
A homeless man making offerings to the after-future
Sculpting rubber tree forests out of worn tires and shoe
soles
A nation unified in exhale
A cloud of smoke
A native pipe ceremony
All the gathered cigarette butts piled in heaps
Snow-covered mountains
Lipsticks smeared and shriveled
Offerings to an afterworld
Tattoo guns and plastic wrappers
Broken zippers and dead-eyed dolls

It's all overwhelming me, oak and elming me
I have seeded a forest of myself
Little books from tall trees
It matters not what this paper be made of
Give me notebooks made of human flesh
Dried on steel hooks and nooses
Make uses of use, uses of us
It's all overwhelming me, oak and elming me
I have seeded a forest of myself
Little books from tall trees
On bended knee
Prostrate before an altered tree
I've made the forest suit me
Tables and chairs
Papers and prayers
Matter vs. spirit

∞

Yo, the mosh pit
Is star lit
I see the light
In your eyes
Find my way
To the amp
And stage dive
Into your lives

∞

I am as ignorant
As I am heaven-sent

My mind's a circus tent
I ride the elephant
Into the record store
Its foot breaks through the floor
I hear the surface pop
And underneath, the rock
Down in the underground
A more familiar sound
I do a somersault
Into a sonic vault
I'm in the listening booth
On a quest for truth
I nod my head and goof
I shake and move

∞

Everything you see
Tilted to the sea
Everything you touch
Wilted more than once
Everything you know
Melted in the snow
You are all alone
You are all aglow
No one has to know

∞

Future slave narrative
Comparative literature

Sketches of an undeveloped picture
Charcoal star soul
I Ching detected from a bar code
Download mad niggas by the carload
A brief history of timelessness borrowed
King of sorrow/ King pleasure
Buried treasure
Twelfth Night/ Measure for Measure
Paranoid Android
Listen at your leisure
Or beat it, Michael Jackson
Red leather

Disfigured nigga
Inbred communion
Remnants of a resurrected ruin
Pray with your eyes closed
Sleep with your door closed
We want to see those truths that you're hiding

Bride in a white dress
Cried in her white dress
Salt-water moon daughter
Bled at her ritual
Communion
Same blood
Different visual

Digital ritual

Ritual digital

Binary star

Some cats in a car

Rollin on dubs

Do you know where your kids are?

Rollin with thugs

Drinkin that good shit

Smokin dem drugs

We got you tied up

Brain sleazed and fried up

Eyelids are pried up

You see what I see?

White mothafuckas tryin to be what I be

Black mothafuckas tryin to shop to feel free

∞

I'm waiting to board an airplane in Atlanta when I spot Hype Williams. We greet each other and begin catching up. I ask him if he knows about the long list of songs that was sent to radio programmers, suggesting that those songs not be played. He was unaware. I tell him that no rap songs were on the list, primarily because the vast majority of mainstream rappers are not talking about anything of any political relevance, nothing that might counter the system in any way. In fact, rap radio feeds the economy. He tells me that the rap game is like fast food and that people will always want fast food. He asks me if I listen to hip-hop. I tell him that I study it, but that I cannot listen to it in most cases for the same reason I don't eat meat: I don't like how it feels in my system. I tell him that I can't listen to it because it seems to betray the hip-hop that molded me. He wants to know if I remember Public Enemy, KRS, Rakim . . . I tell him that I have difficulty listening to contemporary hip-hop because I can't forget.

> "Maybe you should search reality and / stop wishing for beats
> and steady bass / and lyrics said in haste / if its meaning
> doesn't manifest / put it to rest"

"POETRY" KRS-ONE 1987

Hype and I seem to symbolize different worlds with the same last name. He is in first class and I am in economy, in the back (keeping it real?). We are balancing the plane by sitting in our respective seats. Our respective films *Slam* and *Belly* came out the same October day three years ago. We are both playing our roles in doing what we feel we were put here to do. The pilot has just announced that we are at 10,000 feet and that the movie will be *Cats & Dogs*. Funny. This makes me think of the magazine cover I just read that says "DMX: Hip-hop's Hardest Rapper." DMX was the star of *Belly*. If I were to figure into the rap equation, I'd probably be the softest. To most dogs I'm probably a pussy. Back to Hype. Hype is not a rapper, yet I feel he has contributed greatly to what now is represented as hip-hop culture through the media. And I guess even more importantly, young black culture. The question I am posed, as an artist who is very much a critic of hip-hop and popular culture, is whether I am most comfortable preaching to the converted or, more accurately, what would I say if I had the opportunity to sit and talk with a Jay-Z, a DMX, or a rap entity who reaches the mainstream on a regular basis?

One might ask, well, who the fuck am I to criticize, especially when I'm on some poetry shit. Well, actually my love of poetry didn't happen because I grew up reading poetry but because I grew up with very strong doses of hip-hop and that is the poetry that shaped me and molded me. Through hip-hop I gained my biggest appreciation of myself and my culture. Hip-hop made me proud to be black in ways that my parents could never do by forcing me to read a Langston Hughes poem. And even when I began writing poems in the mid-'90s, while everyone started going on and on about who was producing what (Dre's beats, Premier's hooks, etc.), I stepped into the poetry arena, which at the time was synonymous with the underground hip-hop scene, because it felt like lyricism was getting the short end of the stick. I wasn't being fulfilled lyrically. Thus, the poetry that I began writing was to fill the void between what I was hearing and what I wanted to hear from hip-hop. I simply decided to take the beat away and focus solely on lyricism. And much of my current dissatisfaction comes from the fact that if I now had to look at hip-hop for inspiration or guidance, I feel as if I might be misled. I don't doubt for a minute that these emcees, with their bandannas and ice, are soldiers. That's exactly what they are. But I can't figure out who's giving the orders, or whether there is any actual order.

So the question remains, what would I say if mainstream rappers were listening? Perhaps I would begin by asking them what would they say, if the whole world were listening? Then I would question whether they were aware of the fact that the world was listening and responding to all that they said. . . .

We are defined by our ability to resonate and shape sounds. Word. Therefore what we say is of the utmost importance. What we say matters (becomes matter). That is why the spiritual communities have always had people recite prayers and mantras aloud, because they know that they will affect global consciousness and reality itself. We seem to have once, subconsciously, known that in hip-hop as well. Our earliest slang, "word," "word up," "word life," "word is bond," all seemed to revel in this knowledge. As Guru said, "These are the words that I manifest." We nodded our heads in affirmation and then when Biggie named his first album *Ready to Die* we all acted surprised when it happened. Word is bond, son. Plain and simple.

How much senseless violence have we spoken of without taking into account the possibility of our calling these things into existence? Emcees, there is a power in words. There is a power in sound vibration. It affects reality. In fact, it determines it. Hip-hop is much more powerful than mere party music. I don't mean to bring no hateration to the dancerie, but hip-hop, because of its hard drumbeats and conversational chants and rhymes, has the power of any sacred ritual. It is no coincidence that it has reshaped and redefined youth culture, globally. I am not suggesting that we not aim to depict our realities through our music, but we should also realize that we shape our realities as we depict them.

Why is it that if you flipped to BET during the World Trade

Center incident it was showing videos when every other station was showing news? It stood out like a metaphoric commentary on the relevance of contemporary black music. Is the latest and most important news in the black community that Jay-Z and Puffy have gotten off free while we remain enslaved to their senseless ideas and lack of ideals. In the latest Bad Boy release there is a lyric that says, "Bad Boy ain't going nowhere until Tibet is free." Why would anyone align himself with the type of oppression that keeps the Dalai Lama from being able to return to his homeland? You may ask why I am calling the names of a few rappers, as if they are to blame, I am not placing blame, I am simply raising questions. The fact of the matter is that there are no famous philosophers or thinkers in this day and age. There are merely famous entertainers. Yet we associate with them by their philosophy. If you believe that "bitches ain't shit," you know who to listen to. If you're a hustler or a playa, you know who to listen to. But when we sing along with a song, are we operating off of our highest principles, or are we saying things that we would take back if we thought seriously about it? And what if you don't take it back? Is word still bond? Are these the words we manifest? Are these the prayers and mantras of our community? Are we determining an unchanging reality by focusing on keeping it real? We are not powerless. We do live and speak with the power of determining our realities and affecting our environment both positively and negatively. Hip-hop at its best was strategic, and the strategy at that time was about a bit more than getting paid. The problem is that we are ignoring the lessons that we learned from KRS,

Public Enemy, Rakim, Jungle Brothers, Queen Latifah and other golden age rap groups that revolutionized hip-hop. It has been said that those who do not know their history are bound to repeat it. It seems that hip-hop is in the midst of either re-learning or forgetting lessons that have already been taught. But don't get me wrong. This is not a plea to rappers or whomever to become more conscious of what they say; this is not someone trying to enlighten minds. This is a prediction. If you are in some way affiliated with any of these emcees getting airplay, or polluting your airspace with their lack of insight, I would advise you to begin reading aloud. Your shit will not last. You will manifest your truths and die in the face of them. These are your last days. We are growing tired of you. We love women for more than you have ever seen in them. We love hip-hop for more than you have ever used it for. We love ourselves, not for our possessions, but for the spirit that possesses us. We honor your existence. We honor your freedom. But a freedom that costs, obviously, is not free. Watch what you say. Watch what you value. Planes crash. Bank vaults are airtight, you will suffocate in them. Cars crash. Word life. Word death. Your hit songs hit and run. We are wounded but not dead. And we are coming to reclaim what is ours. The main stream: the ocean. The current. Our time is now. Word is bond.

ACKNOWLEDGMENTS

I acknowledge that I am a vessel pressed against the lips of the Faceless. I am an instrument in a symphony orchestrated by the hands of an electrifying conductor. I am thankful to play my part. I am a part of the plan. Just like you. I acknowledge your presence, kiss your eyes and thank you for being. It's going to be fun getting to know each other. Let's have an open relationship. Just kidding. Never more than you and I.

I also acknowledge the hands, hearts, and minds that graced the trail from my hands to yours. They have been instrumental. All parts are equal. We give and take. But those who give of themselves in the name of another are of the highest rank. I thank you with all of my heart. Your devotion to your work and craft has intensified my devotion to my own. Thank you for planning, proofing, laying out, marketing, researching, and outlining a dream now manifest.

Finally, I would like to acknowledge that I am neither here nor there. I am not what you think. Only what you know in your heart. I believe in you and trust you can feel me. But, truly, I'm just that NGH you may cross the street to avoid, invested with love and a nurturing family. Some are not as lucky. All are blessed. Feel me? We use what we got . . .

My man Kwam told me, "Ain't no use. NGHs are broken." Nah man, NGHs ain't broken. NGHs are broken-hearted. Ain't no love in the promise land. Ain't that a BCH! My love told me that she had to learn how to surrender to love again after her divorce. But first she had to allow herself time to heal. NGHs are healin. That's why some of 'em be wearin

Band-Aids, buying themselves diamonds and speaking of their worth. We were once worthless. Never forget, regardless of how much it breaks your heart or strains your imagination to remember. We served life as if trialed by God: slavery. Capital punishment. Got way too many emcees serving sentences. Word is bond. The source and power of your wordplay is no game. Playas beware. Game recognize truth. I love y'all more than words. I can't say it enough. Shit, so much I've made expressing that love my hustle, my daily bread. And, nah, NGHs may not be broken, but I've sure been broke (Big shout out to the heads that be helping me manage my scrilla!). And I acknowledge the wit and savvy of all you hustlers that had to do what you had to do to not be broke. Now, let's do what we got to do to not be broken. Let's learn to love again: our mothers, our children, ourselves. And let's let that love resonate through our music (That doesn't mean I ain't goin to check out Three6Mafia tonight, 'cause I am. Believe it. If Project Pat is there I'm gonna lose it!). Balance. We walk the fine line between now and the eternal. Our journey has the makings of scripture. Which ain't much more than souped up poetry (yes, of course, inspired by the divine).

What is a poem's worth? You decide. Recite me off page or know me by heart. I am written. So be it. I acknowledge that I am not the first, nor will I be the last, but I am here and now. And in this moment I acknowledge that we are all much more than ourselves. We are each other. And together we are part of a universe. One verse of a poem that extends beyond before and after. I know nothing of the author except that I love her. I feel kissed by language, let alone by my love.

Dear Creator/Destroyer Dimension, thank you for life and for name. We live our signature to sign your treaty. Feathers in inkwells, we bleed through paper. May our testament fulfill thy will. Hallelujah! Dollar, dollar bill, y'all!

And I'm out.

SAUL WILLIAMS AKA NIGGY TARDUST

Live from Tinsel Town
(Recorded in front of a dead audience.)

October 17, 2005